Shattered Like Me

D. DUQUETTE

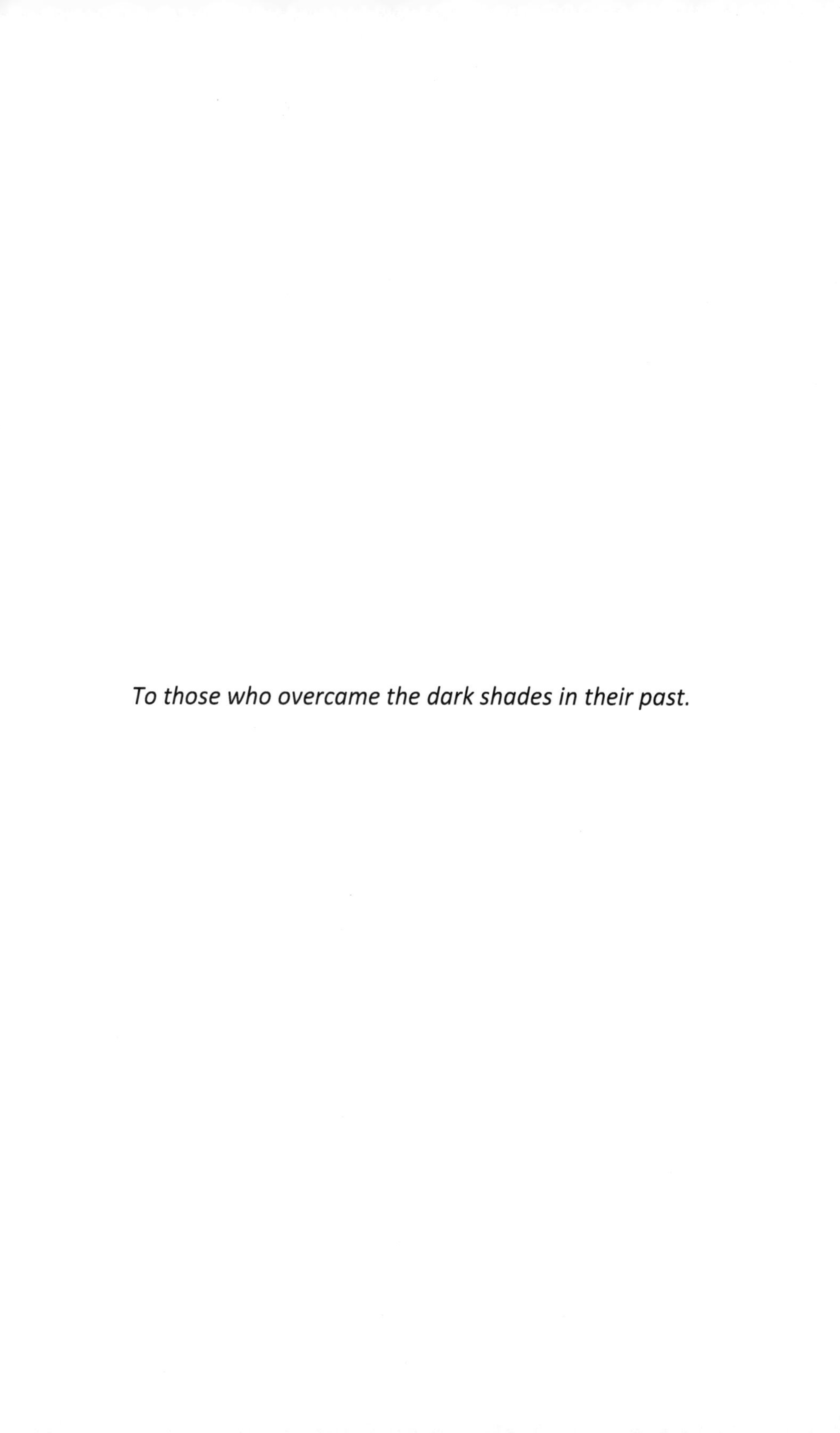

To those who overcame the dark shades in their past.

CHAPTER ONE

I wondered what it was like to live the luxurious life of an adult. Okay, not just any adult, a well-established one. As I look around, I say a silent prayer to myself that someday my life will be like this. I want the inground pool and outdoor kitchen. I want the hot tub and outdoor shower.

This is my third time sitting this house, but I'm just as excited as the first day I had this place all to myself. I hopped from one lounge chair to the next. After a half hour, I walked around the pool and tested out the lounge chairs on the other side. If anyone was watching, then surely they'd think I was crazy.

I was just a high school graduate who loved nothing more than pretending to be somebody I wasn't. I started this business the summer before my junior year when my teacher needed someone to look after her house while she taught a summer class abroad in Ireland. Yes, I'd much rather be in Ireland than boring Missouri, but having a four-bedroom house all to myself at sixteen years old was just as glamorous.

I know what you're thinking...house party. Well, you would need friends for that. I had one friend named Jesse since we were in kindergarten. Besides, I wouldn't want to ruin my outstanding reputation with my teachers. Through word of mouth, I was house sitting every school break we had although the summers were my favorite.

This summer wouldn't be any different. My first house would only be for a month and then I had two options lined up to end my summer. I could stay here in Missouri and house sit for two more months or I could go out of state, to Texas to sit for an old teacher who moved there. I really loved the idea of getting out of this state only I didn't have a car. My brother was home from college and just like every year he would take the car until he went back to school again.

Every time I talked about getting my own car, my mother told me I'd be off to college before I knew it so to try and make it work with my brother. There was no working...he was older, he got the car twenty-four seven and I got shafted, asking Jesse to tote me around when I needed a lift. The truth was, I wasn't going to college, but my mother had no idea. It was a conversation I didn't care to have just yet. I wanted to travel and see the world, house sitting internationally. I didn't want to rack up thousands of dollars in student loans and start out in debt up to my eyeballs. I wanted to start adulthood by having the time of my life.

After a dip in the pool I made myself some pasta salad. I ate the entire heaping bowl and then chastised myself for eating too much that I wasn't able to move. After ten minutes of entertaining myself by puffing out my belly to make myself look pregnant, I popped the cork on a bottle of wine and sunk into the hot tub. *Mmm...this wine is good.* My teacher's husband made it and although I am too young to drink, I took her smile with a wink as she slid the bottle across the table as a green light.

"St. Louis Police Department, open up," I heard a deep voice say. *Shoot! I'm drinking and I'm not twenty-one!* I heard the gate begin to open so I quickly jumped up, knocking over the glass of wine as I hopped over the side of the hot tub, stepping on the broken glass. *Shit! Oh, that hurts...that hurts.* I bent down to check my foot. There was already blood all over the cement.

"Hello? St. Louis Police Department."

I popped up, startling the officer. He was young, too young to have such a deep voice.

"H...h...hi." I was a stuttering idiot, completely memorized by his malachite eyes. I had never seen anyone with iris's so alluring. I read somewhere green eyes were the rarest.

"Hello miss. We just received a phone call about a noise complaint."

"Ahhh..."

"Do you mind if I have a look around?" he asked.

For what?

"Okay..." I stood there dripping wet in my bright purple bikini with the bottom of my foot on fire. I watched the officer as he walked around to where I was standing, his facial expression changing when the broken glass and blood came into view.

"What's going on?" he demanded.

"I...it's...you just scared the shit out of me. I was sitting here relaxing and then I hear police and I jumped up knocking my glass of wine over and then it broke, but I didn't realize what I had done before it was too late and I stepped all over the glass. My foot is killing me right now and I'm scared to move because I don't know what I did or if I'm in trouble right now. I'm not twenty-one yet so I'm not supposed to be drinking so I'm freaking out you're going to arrest me. This isn't my house..."

"Easy, easy. Slow down. There was no noise complaint...it was just a joke. This is my aunt's house. She told me someone would be here watching her house while she was gone."

"Are you serious right now?" I asked, stepping away from the glass and finding the closest chair to sit in. I wrapped my arms over my chest to shield my body.

"Yeah. I thought she was leaving tomorrow. I just stopped by to say goodbye before she left and ask if she needed anything."

"She left yesterday. I'll let her know you stopped by if she calls," I said, annoyed.

"You realize you're bleeding pretty good right now?"

"I know. I'm waiting for you to leave."

"You're not too friendly, are you?"

"Actually, I am a very friendly person. I'm just..."

"Nervous?"

"Yes. Am I in trouble? I just had a sip. I'll dump the rest of the bottle out."

Oh great, now he's laughing at me.

"Sorry. My smile means no disrespect to you. You're just kind of...adorable? And no, I don't arrest underage girls for taking a sip of wine while house sitting."

"So, you're just going to take my word for it? I could be on my second bottle by now," I blurted out, forgetting who I was talking to. His smirk disappeared.

"Don't push your luck," he said.

"I apologize. I don't know why I just said that. I swear I just took one sip and I promise I won't pour another glass."

"Maybe you need to...you seem very uptight."

"I don't care for police officers," I blurted out.

LIAR!*Why did I just say that? Arrrrgghhh!*

"And why's that?" he questioned.

"I just don't."

"I'll be right back," he said, turning and leaving through the gate. I couldn't see beyond the six-foot wooden panel fencing. *Oh great, I'm in trouble now. I can't believe I just told him I didn't like him.* I flipped my foot over, finding a piece of glass stuck in the arch. My stomach turned. I was okay with blood, but not this much. My foot was starting to go numb. I jumped when the officer returned.

"I'm officer Mac by the way. What's your name?" he asked, kneeling before me and unzipping a small navy blue pouch.

"Clara...Clara Kate."

"Hi Clara Kate."

"Hi," I smiled, watching him take a pair of tweezers out.

"You have a piece of glass..."

"I know. I'm feeling kind of queasy. I think I need to lay down."

"Okay, here," he said, reaching out his arm for me to grab onto. I took it, glancing at everything he had on his waist. Handcuffs, pepper spray, flashlight and a gun were all I could see before he had me walking to the lounge chair. I laid down.

"Are you feeling dizzy at all?"

"I'm okay."

"That's not an answer."

"A little dizzy."

"Okay. Hold tight to the arm of the chair and squeeze it if it hurts. I can see the glass, it's a good size. Ready?"

"Okay."

"One, two, three."

OW!

"How was that?"

"Fantastic!"

"Oh, you're sarcastic. I never would've thought," he smirked. I sat up grinning at him.

"One-nine, are you there? One-nine," the radio on Mac's shoulder came to life.

"One-nine, here," Mac said, holding down the button on the side of his walkie talkie.

"I need your location."

"Two ten Squirrel Run."

Liar!It's five Squirrel Run, not even close.

"I have a call about a suspicious female in the parking lot of Radio. Blue Subaru. Caller said car's been idling for quite some time."

"Okay," he said and turned to me. I studied his face while he grabbed some gauze and wrapped his warm hand around my foot. The contact made my heart skip an extra beat, along with the fact that his chiseled jawline and defined cheekbones were very strong. *And perfect!*

"You okay?" he asked.

"I'm not going to pass out, if that's what you're worried about."

"Not at all. Your ghostly white look is now turning lobster red. Are you blushing right now?"

"Go check on your suspicious female...I'm fine...really!" *Ugh, just go!*

"Here, use this. I'll be right back to check on you. If not, I'll swing by when I get off at eleven. I'll see you later," he said before I could even protest. I'm sure his aunt had all this first aid stuff in her house and I definitely didn't need him checking on me! I'd be in bed by eleven. *Errr.*

I finished cleaning up my foot and made my way inside to find a paper bag to put the glass in. I could barely put any pressure on my foot. I have a five-mile run I had signed up for early next week in honor of my niece who died from SIDS. *I better be able to run!* I hadn't missed a year since she passed four years ago.

After I cleaned up the glass, I took a wet towel to scrub at the blood and wine. I grabbed a bucket of hot tub water and wrung out my towel, scrubbing until the mess was gone. I flipped the hot tub cover back over the hot tub, pissed that Mac had ruined my plans for a relaxing evening.

I didn't like meeting new people and I especially didn't like police officers. They meant trouble and I steered far away from any and all trouble. I sulked like a child back into the house with my head hung low, tossing all the trash away and plopping onto the couch. *Shoot, I'm still in my wet bathing suit!* I got off the couch, knowing full well my teacher would not appreciate me sprawled across her ten-person sofa in a wet bathing suit. I changed into my booty shorts and a tank top, grabbing the TV remote on my way by the coffee table.

I wasn't a huge fan of television. *How could anyone sit through an entire series of watching someone catching fish or mining for gold?* BORING! I liked shows that were completely different from one episode to the next. I landed on a murder mystery show. That would do. The first story was about a serial killer who tied women up and showered them before he killed them. The second was about a man who murdered his wife and buried her in the driveway the day before a crew showed up to pave it with asphalt. *Wow, talk about genius*. The only problem was his neighbor woke in the middle of the night to the sound of him digging her hole with his shovel and came forward when he heard the woman was missing. Just as I was learning the background to the third story, there was a knock on the door. I was so engrossed in the television, I jumped at the noise.

I checked the time, just past eleven o'clock. *Officer Mac*.

"Officer Mac," I said, trying to hide my annoyance.

"Jack."

"Mac Jack?"

"Jack Mac, but you can just call me Jack, Clara Kate." The way he said my name sent shivers down my spine.

"Sit," he ordered.

"Excuse me?"

"I just saw you hobble over here through the glass panel on the side of the door. I want to check out your foot. I feel really bad about earlier."

"I'm fine, honestly. Here's your first aid kit back. Thank you for letting me borrow it."

"No problem," he said, making his way inside and plopping down on the couch. He placed his arm up behind his head and made himself right at home.

"Sooo?" I asked, not wanting to entertain him. I just wanted to take my sour mood to bed knowing tomorrow would be a new day.

"I'm sorry. Am I interrupting...?" he looked at the television. "Your murder show?"

"No. I'm just tired," I replied, yawning.

"I've seen this one. The guy gets robbed on his walk to the grocery store...gunned down for a measly twenty-dollar bill."

Jack must have seen the exasperated look on my face because he apologized for ruining the ending to the story. Any thoughts of Jack being obnoxious were multiplying by the minute.

"I forgot you don't like cops because we're all trouble," he said, getting up from the couch and walking down the hall to the bathroom. I hobbled back over to the couch and sat down, waiting for Mac Jack to return.

"Better?" I heard Jack ask. I looked up to see him in his bathing suit. I felt my cheeks heat and wanted to bury my face in the cushion. "What?" he asked. I had never seen a man this beautiful with broad shoulders and a sculptured chest. My eyes wandered down to his taut abs. *What is happening to me right now? Please God let me keep my composure.*

"What are you doing?" I asked.

"I took my uniform off so we can pretend I'm not an officer and you can play nice. I'm just going to take a dip in my aunt's hot tub if that's okay with you."

"Do you normally come here late at night to do this?"

"Actually, I do, but just on the nights I work. It's relaxing for me."

"Does your aunt know?"

"Of course. She tells me to come by any time. She and my uncle are usually sleeping by the time I get off, but I'm quiet. Do you want to join me?"

"Definitely not. A few hours earlier when I tried to enjoy the hot tub, things didn't end so well."

"I'm really sorry. Honestly, I feel terrible."

"I'm going to bed. Will you lock up when you leave?" I asked, trying desperately not to show how affected I had become by this strange man's beauty.

"Sure."

"Thanks," I said, shutting off the tv and hobbling to the stairs. Jack stood there watching me. When I turned to face him, he told me to have a good night and left the room. He was aggravating, walking around like he owned the place. This was my place! Well, for the next month.

I climbed the stairs and brushed my teeth before heading to the guest bedroom. I peeked out the window, finding Jack relaxing in the hot tub with his back to me. *Wow…talk about muscular*. He had a giant tattoo on his back, but I couldn't make out what it said. It almost looked like wings. Part of me wanted to venture downstairs and get to know Jack a little more, but the other part of me knew better.

Jack had tattoos which meant he had stories…history. People only tattooed themselves when they had a story to tell and the bigger the tattoo, the more painful the story was. I wasn't up for story time. I mean, I certainly wasn't ready to tell mine.

CHAPTER TWO

I walked to the nearest hardware store and bought a lock for the back gate. *There!* Jack won't be able to burst through all cop happy anymore. My foot felt fine when I woke up, but now it was throbbing again. I spent the rest of the day with it propped up, icing it on and off throughout the day.

I called my best friend Jesse.

"Hello?"

"Hey! Are you still picking me up Thursday?" I asked.

"What's Thursday?"

"Jesse!"

"Kidding, I'm kidding! I'll be there at nine in the morning."

"Eight thirty."

"The race doesn't start until ten, Clara Kate."

"I know, but I need to check-in, get my number and then warm up."

"Whatever you say! Eight thirty it is!"

"Thanks Jesse! I'll see you in a couple of days."

"Love you girl."

"Love you too."

By the time race day arrived, my foot was feeling much better. I bandaged it up more than usual and stood by the door waiting for Jesse. She showed right on time. I practically ran to her car. During school we saw each other every day, but in the summer we were so busy doing other things.

"Hi!" I said, giving her a big hug.

"Look at you, girl. You're not supposed to look so sexy when you're just going to sweat," Jesse teased, backing down the driveway.

"What about you? Where are your running clothes?"

"I decided not to run anymore. Chad asked me to go to a baseball game with him tomorrow and if I run today, I know I'll be dead for our date."

"Date?"

"I think so! He's been texting me a lot lately."

"See that, absence makes the heart grow fonder. Now that he's not seeing you in school anymore..."

"Exactly!"

"Well, I'm really sad I'll be running all alone."

"Oh, who are you kidding? I'd never be able to keep up with you anyways. Here's twenty bucks towards your goal," she said, handing me the folded bill.

"Thanks! I almost met my goal this year," I beamed.

"What was it?"

"Four hundred. Just needed twenty more."

"Here's my purse," she said, grabbing her bag from the backseat as she drove and placing it on my lap. "Just take twenty more from my wallet."

"No way! You're going to college in the fall. You will need every penny!"

"It means more to me that you will meet your goal. Trust me!"

"Is this just guilt money? If so, I'm not taking it. I mean, you probably wouldn't have been able to keep up with me anyway."

"You bitch!" she hissed, playfully. "It's not guilt money. It's I want to help my best friend money. Now just take it before I change my mind!" I started laughing. Jesse was the greatest best friend anyone could ever ask for. She hated running, but she always supported my love for it.

Jesse stood in line with me to get my number and then helped me warm up. Just before the race started, she told me she would meet me at the finish line. I was all pumped up to run. I looked at the picture of my baby niece right before the shot fired and then I took off, keeping in mind that this was not an actual race where I had to finish first. I was just running for Madeline.

I thought back to the day Madeline died. My oldest brother and his girlfriend were living with my mother and me at the time. I'll never forget those blood curdling screams from my brother. Madeline was just over four months old. My brother had put her to bed the night before and when my brother's girlfriend woke in the morning, they both ran to Madeline's crib wondering why she had slept through the night. They quickly realized she wasn't breathing. I ran to the bedroom to see my niece. She just looked like she was sleeping. Then my brother picked her up and his girlfriend was screaming at him to put her back down. I ran back to my room and called for an ambulance. Maybe she wasn't dead. Maybe there was still hope.

The paramedics pronounced Madeline dead at the scene. We were all interviewed by the police, asking if I ever saw my brother or his girlfriend act out of character with my niece. Hell, my brother turned into a different person the day she was born. He became nicer for one thing and changed his voice for another, talking to Madeline in this goo goo baby language. Abuse? No way! Madeline was spoiled with love.

The autopsy revealed Madeline died of SIDS, Sudden Infant Death Syndrome. The medical examiner assured all of us there wasn't even a drop of dirt underneath her fingernails. She was cherished and he knew it too.

I tried to hold back the tears as I ran, thinking back to Madeline's services. My brother's girlfriend insisted on an open casket. Her family was Catholic and it was custom to preview the dead body. I took a swift punch to my gut when I saw that tiny casket and another when my eyes landed on my sweet baby Maddy. She was robbed of her life and so was my brother. He hasn't been the same since, especially after his girlfriend blamed him for her death.

He had given Madeline a bath before he put her to bed and his girlfriend swore he got water in her lungs. She was also convinced he placed her on her stomach in the crib and not on her back. I used to adore his girlfriend and now...now I hated her. If losing your own child wasn't enough punishment, then having the love of your life blame you for it sure was.

I thought some more about life and how different things would be if Madeline were still alive. My brother was in Colorado now, crushing the slopes as a snowboard instructor. He moved the same week his girlfriend left him, telling my mother and me he had absolutely nothing to lose.

My foot started to hurt right before the halfway mark and now that I had half a mile left until the finish line, I wondered if I would be finishing at all. The pain radiating up my leg was starting to become unbearable. My leg gave out and I stumbled to the ground, smashing my knee on the asphalt and catching my weight with my hands.

"Are you okay?" a man stopped and knelt down next to me. He wrapped his arms around my waist and pulled me to a standing position.

"Stepped on glass," I panted as people raced by us.

"Oh my gosh. It went through your sneaker?"

"Three days ago. Barefoot. The pain is so bad, but I have to run...for Madeline." He nodded his head.

"I'll try to help you. Just lean on me." I placed my arm around his neck and we started to walk at a fast pace. "My name is Dennis, by the way."

"Clara Kate. Madeline's my niece...well, was. Four months old."

"I run for my son, Benjamin...Benny Boy. He was two months old when my wife found him unresponsive in his bassinet."

"I'm so sorry," I said as I tried desperately to hobble in the direction of the finish line.

"I'm sorry too. Madeline; what a beautiful name."

"She was perfect." I imagine people wondered what in the world we were doing. I'm sure anyone else struggling would have just limped off to the sideline and called it quits, but something inside my soul kept putting one foot in front of the other.

When we passed the finish line, I crumbled to the ground. I was exhausted. It took far more energy trying to run while leaning on someone than actually running, but with much less pain than before. I knew it wasn't an ideal spot to collapse, but knowing I finished and could now catch my breath was the best feeling in the world.

"Are you okay?" Dennis asked.

"Clara Kate! Oh my gosh! Are you okay?" Jesse shrieked.

"I'll be fine. I just have to catch my breath." Together Dennis and Jesse picked me up, carrying me to the side and placing me down on the grass.

"Dennis, my best friend Jesse. Jesse, Dennis." I watched them exchange handshakes, smiling pleasantly at one another.

"What happened? Five miles is usually a piece of cake for you!"

"I know. It's a long story, but I got a cut on my foot a few days ago and I thought I would be okay to run, but halfway through I realized it was a bad idea. I fell and Dennis helped me up and carried me the rest of the way."

"Wow," Jesse exclaimed, looking at Dennis and smiling again.

"I can't thank you enough...seriously. Can I buy you dinner?" I asked.

"Me too," Jesse piped in, all too happy. *I thought she just said she had a date with Chad...*

Just then a woman appeared, linking her arm through Dennis'.

"Hi honey. How was your race?" She had a baby strapped to the front of her and another child by her leg.

"Sweetheart, this is Clara Kate and her friend Jesse. Clara Kate and Jesse, this is my wife Rebecca."

I saw the smile disappear from Jesse's face. Oh, she was definitely interested in Dennis.

"All right, ladies, I better go," he said.

"Wait! How about a picture for keepsake?" I asked, wondering internally if that was odd.

"Sure," Dennis replied. Jesse took out her phone as Dennis and I stood next to each other, smiling for the camera.

"Can I do anything for you as a thank you?" I asked, hoping there was some way I could repay him for his kindness.

"Yeah, run this race again next year...for Madeline AND my Benny Boy."

"Deal! It was nice to meet you and thank you again."

I watched Dennis walk off with his wife. He picked up the little boy and tossed him on top of his shoulders. I instantly wondered what it was like grieving over a child while trying to keep your head in your marriage. Then I wondered if I would ever be a part of a family with children of my own.

"Come on, I'll take you home," Jesse sulked.

"I cannot believe you were eye googling that guy! You really think you're going to find THE one at a SIDS benefit run? And what about your hot date tomorrow?"

"C'mon...he carried you...for how long?"

"I leaned on him for a half mile, Jesse!"

"That is so romantic...and sexy. He was hot!"

"Yeah, he was pretty cute...for being old!"

"How old do you think he was?" she asked.

"I don't know. He didn't say. Why, how old is too old for you to date?"

"I'm a fan of the twice my age rule. I'm eighteen so that would mean anyone under thirty-six. I'd say he qualified."

"Thanks for the math, Jesse. Thirty-six. What in the hell would a thirty-six-year-old have to offer you?"

"A really large, experienced penis," she gushed, the whites of her eyes widening.

"Okay, let's go! Drive me back to Mrs. Penney's house!" I demanded, shaking my head at her and trying to stifle my grin.

"You want to do a sleepover tonight?" Jesse asked.

"Not tonight. I want to sit on the couch and not get back up until tomorrow morning. Raincheck, though?"

"Okay."

We arrived at Mrs. Penney's a few minutes later. Jesse helped me inside and then cooked lunch for me.

"I'm not sick," I said.

"You had a big day. I can't believe you ran with a cut on your foot. You running that five-mile already made me look bad, let alone with an injured foot. You rocked it!"

I sat on the couch after lunch and watched Jesse rummage through Mrs. Penney's house.

"Why do you do this every time? You're going to get me in trouble!"

"Mrs. Penney is just too perfect. I know I'll find something here that lets me know she's not the angel she pretends to be."

"Just don't touch anything."

"You worry too much," Jesse said. After searching and coming up with nothing, she gave her farewell.

"I'll call you after my date with Chad."

"Okay, have fun!"

I felt relieved when Jesse left. I loved her, but she was so darn nosey. Mrs. Penney was a very sweet woman. She helped me a lot through my high school years, so it didn't feel right having her belongings rifled through.

I locked the door and walked straight to the freezer, pulling out some ice and putting it in a plastic Ziploc bag. Then I wrapped it up in a hand towel before sitting back on the couch to ice my foot. After an hour, I got up and hobbled around for some Tylenol and a glass of ice-cold water.

"Shit, Clara Kate. Are you okay?"

I jumped at the sound of a man's deep voice. I blinked my eyes and saw Jack leaning down next to me. It was dark outside now. I must have fallen asleep.

"What are you doing and how did you get in here?" I screeched.

"The back gate was locked so I got worried. I used the spare key," he said, holding up a key. I snatched it out of his hand.

"Sorry. I didn't mean to startle you," he said. "What is your deal?"

"You! I'm the one your aunt chose to watch her house, not you! You just can't come barging in here whenever you feel like it."

"You're acting like I'm some kind of asshole right now. The gate is always open and then when I found a lock on it, I got concerned..."

"I put the lock on there so YOU would STAY OUT!"

"All right...I get it. I'll leave you alone. Jeez!" he said, with his arms up in surrender. He turned to walk back out the door.

"How do I even know you are who you say you are?" I asked. He dug into his pocket, pushed some buttons and held the phone up to his ear.

"What are you doing? You're going to call the cops on me and try to say I'm trespassing?"

"Aunty, how are you?"

"You called your aunt! It's past eleven o'clock at night!" I hissed, crossing my arms in defense. "Now you're an asshole!" I whispered.

"Clara Kate would like to talk to you," he said, handing me the phone.

"Hi Mrs. Penney."

"Is everything okay?" she asked. Her voice was always such a pleasant sound.

"Oh yes, everything is fine. I'm so sorry Jack called you this late." I gave Jack the dirtiest look I could muster. "I guess he comes here after his shift to relax in your hot tub, but I thought I would be the only one here while you were gone. That's all."

"I hope he isn't bothering you. I told Jack he could use the pool and hot tub any time. I can talk to him for you and just ask him to wait until we return if you'd feel more comfortable with that."

Errrr!

"Oh no, it's no problem at all. I was just making sure he is who he says he is."

"No need to worry. Jack is a wonderful young man. Please be kind to him...he needs it right now more than ever, Clara Kate. Okay?"

What the hell is that supposed to mean?

"Okay. Have a good night and sorry again for bothering you."

"You too," she said, just before I hit the red circle button on Jack's phone. I was beyond irritated now. Jack started smirking as I handed his phone back to him.

"I'd love nothing more than to punch you in the face right now. You're lucky you're a cop."

"Why do you let me bother you so much?"

"I don't like people," I said, hobbling to the stairs. "I just like being alone."

"Why?" he asked, looking perplexed.

"Everybody has a story and I'm tired of listening to them. Let me guess...you have a story too...a big one to match your big tattoo on your back. You're tainted...I already know it. Your aunt just told me to be nice to you and it's clear you're looking for a friend, but it's not going to be me. So why don't you leave the way you came in and come back in approximately three weeks and three days when I AM GONE?!"

The look on Jack's face made me realize I had laid into him a little too hard. He turned around and walked out the door without a word.

"Thank you," I hollered, just before the door closed. *Wow, I was such a bitch! Maybe I was getting my period.* I shut off the lights in the living room and peered out the back sliding glass door. I could see Jack taking off his uniform and neatly placing it on Mrs. Penney's outdoor table.

My eyes were fixed on his tattoo, even when Jack was completely naked. Okay, I took a peek at his bum, but then my eyes wandered back up. There were two angel wings, one on either side that went down his entire back. In the middle was a figure...a baby swaddled in a blanket. There were numbers at the bottom...2.14.12-6.2.15.

Upon another glance, I saw ***My Son*** in cursive writing just over the baby's head. Jack didn't need to tell me his story. It was right there, permanently inked on his skin...probably too painful to tell. I watched Jack sink down into the hot tub and started feeling like I should go apologize to him. I too had a story...everybody did. Maybe I was just tired of feeling the pain from hearing them because I still wasn't ready to deal with my own.

I slid the back door open and Jack looked up at me.

"I get it, I'm leaving. I just had a really shitty night and apparently, I should've just gone home. Instead I came here where it just got shittier."

I hobbled over to a lounge chair and wheeled it next to the hot tub.

"Can we start over? I'm Clara Kate," I said, leaning on the hot tub and extending my hand over to Jack. He hesitated, making my insides start to squirm and then shook it, hiding his amusement. I too was grinning now.

"Jack."

"Hi Jack. I'm in a bad mood because I tried to run a five mile today for a really good cause, but I failed miserably. See, I probably shouldn't have been running at all because I stepped on a piece of glass that cut my foot. That is a long story in itself, though..."

"I have time," he interrupted. "Please tell me how you cut your foot."

"Seriously?" I asked, smiling at Jack. I ran my hand through the water.

"What happened?"

"Well, I was relaxing in this very hot tub, minding my own business when I heard an officer at that gate, right there," I said, pointing to the gate. "I'm eighteen and I was drinking a glass of wine, so I was going to jump out and dump it before I let him in. I did things a little backwards, though. I dumped the glass of wine and then jumped on top of it."

"So did you get in trouble with the cop?"

"No."

"Sounds like a really nice guy. You know, he could've arrested you right on the spot."

I rolled my eyes at him.

"So what did you think about this police officer? Girls think they are pretty sexy in their uniform and all."

"Nope...not me," I lied. Sexy didn't even come close to how attractive Jack truly was.

"What if this cop wasn't wearing his uniform? What if he wasn't a cop? Would you like him then?"

"Maybe." *PROBABLY!*

"You have a very combative personality. Has anyone ever told you that?"

"No, Jack. That would be the first...thank you for that."

"Sorry. It's just, you don't like cops and you don't like meeting new people. Then there's the fact that you don't like listening to your body when it's telling you to just sit and relax. Instead, you run five miles? Really?"

"Sitting now," I said, falling back onto the lounge chair and crossing my legs.

"Jeez, Clara Kate, your bandage is all bloody. Did you change it when you got home?"

"No...I haven't had the time."

"You need to take care of it! That cut was pretty deep," he said, getting out of the hot tub and grabbing a towel to dry off.

"I can do it."

"Apparently not." I sighed as I watched Jack go into the house and come back out with some hydrogen peroxide, a small tube of ointment and bandages.

"Queasy?" he asked.

"No."

"This looks pretty bad. I think it's infected."

"Queasy now," I said, laying down.

"This might sting a bit. Ready?"

"Just be done with it," I huffed, right before I felt the cold liquid on the bottom of my foot. "Oh God have mercy that fucking stings!"

"It doesn't look good at all." I squeezed Jack's arm until the pain subsided. I heard Jack opening the bandage and felt his warm hands wrap around my foot. *Why did I feel like I was losing control every time this man touched me?*

"Try that and if it still isn't getting any better by tomorrow, I think you need to go to the doctor."

"Thank you, Officer Mac."

"You're a wise ass."

"Tell me your story," I said, sitting up.

"No. I know what you're doing. You're feeling bad that you keep shutting me down when all I am trying to do is help. It's okay."

"No, really. I saw your tattoo and I want to know about it."

"Then you probably saw my ass, too," he snickered. "What did you think about that?"

"That you could've just used the bathroom inside to change."

"Yeah, I'll get right on that as you chase me out of the house like some guard dog."

"I want to start over. Your tattoo..." Jack turned away from me so I could just see his side. He placed his elbows on his knees and dropped his head into his hands.

"Maybe story time can be another night. I better get going," he said.

"My girl's name was Madeline. Well, she wasn't mine...she was my niece, but she sure felt like mine. The second I held her in my arms, it was like this whole different feeling I never knew awoke inside my heart. Honestly, I had no idea I was even capable of having those feelings. It was pure love. She lived down the hall from me. I would tip toe in there while she was sleeping and just watch her. Madeline was the most beautiful sight my eyes had ever seen." Jack looked up at me just in time to see my tears fall. I wiped them away and swallowed down the pain I've tried so hard to hide.

"She passed away at four months. I never knew how Madeline was able to take up such a big spot in my heart in such a short period of time," I chuckled. "Oh, that girl...she was precious. When she saw me, she would get this big smile on her face. It made me feel so loved. SIDS...she died of SIDS. That's the cause I was running for today."

Jack turned his body to face me now.

"I'm sorry," he said.

"Thanks."

"Jamison, that was his name. He was born my senior year of high school. Truthfully, I didn't want him. His mom and I were just messing around and she was going off to college. I resented Jamison because he ruined my junior and senior year. Junior because that's when she told me she was pregnant. I remember I was just freaking out. She was calmer than I was.

I was relieved when she told me she was giving him up for adoption and then my senior year was ruined when my parents were the ones to adopt him. Instead of going to senior prom, I was busy shopping with my mother for burp clothes and a diaper pail. But all that resentment that had built up over time disappeared the first time I laid eyes on Jamison. I couldn't believe I helped create him. How was that possible? Those tiny fingers and toes...how did I make that? I couldn't wrap my head around it.

Anyway, I tried my best to be a father to him, but my mother took care of him a lot. Jamison's biological mother was away at college. She'd post pictures all the time at parties and sometimes I was jealous. Other times I didn't know how she could pretend she didn't have a son out there in the world that she should be caring for.

I hadn't seen or talked to her since Jamison's birth...well, until he died. He was three years old. He was such a sweet little boy, always running to the door when I got home from work and wanting to be held. I loved him so much," Jack choked. I scooted closer to him and held his hand. "Sorry. I'm just not used to telling many people."

"So that's why your aunt told me to be nice to you."

"No...I wish," he chuckled, wiping the tears from his eyes.

"You mean, there's more to your story?"

"Oh yeah, Jamison is just the beginning."

"Tell me," I urged, my voice a whisper.

"You're confusing, you know that? You tell me I have some big story to tell and you don't want to hear it..."

"I know. I'm sorry. I have my guard up with everyone...it's not just you."

"Oh, so you're the one with the long story."

"Why should I be nice to you, Jack?" I persisted, waiting patiently for him to answer.

"My fiancé left me two weeks ago...at the altar."

"You mean, that stuff really happens?"

"I guess so. Surprisingly, there's no other guy. I mean, truthfully, I wish there was this other guy so I could hate her."

"Then why did she leave?"

"She just thought we wanted different things in life. I wanted to settle down and have a family in the near future. She wanted to travel the world before settling down. I can't just go travel the world."

"She literally waited until what...the pastor had her say 'I do?'"

"Just about. We started saying our vows and then she stopped and told me she couldn't go through with it. Then she ran off down the aisle. It was like a scene right out of a movie."

"Wow."

"Yeah. Now I have no clue what the hell I'm going to do. We bought a house together so I'm getting it ready to put on the market. She moved in with her friend."

"Where are you going to go?"

"I don't know, but I certainly don't need a four-bedroom house when I'm living all by myself. I'm looking for something much smaller."

"I'm so sorry. That's horrible. How long were you two together for?"

"Three years. I met her right after Jamison passed. She saved me from a really dark place and I'll forever be thankful to her for that. I just wish she had told me how she felt before I spent thousands of dollars on a wedding."

"Sounds like she did you a favor. I mean, at least she saved you from a long drawn out divorce."

"I guess."

"Can I ask you how Jamison died?"

"If you tell me your story."

"Maybe someday. I'm just not ready yet."

"What? I just told you so much about my personal life!"

I sat there staring at my knotted fingers. There was no way I was telling him.

"Does it have anything to do with your dislike for cops?"

I nodded my head.

"I hope someday you're able to see that I am not the enemy."

"Me too."

"Well, I better go, but I'll be by tomorrow."

"You don't have to play big brother to me," I told him, walking back inside the house and turning to stand in the doorway.

"And you don't always have to make me feel unwelcome."

"Do I do that?"

"You just did. Just say 'okay, I'll see you tomorrow' and let that be that."

"Jack, I cannot wait to see you tomorrow. I will be waiting by the door. In fact, I think I'll sleep by the door tonight..." I said, sarcastically.

"Forget it."

"I'll see you tomorrow. I'm looking forward to it," I said, smiling at Jack. A part of me enjoyed driving him crazy.

"Goodnight," he said, before I slid the door closed.

CHAPTER THREE

The next morning Jack knocked on the door carrying a grocery bag.

"Good morning, Officer Mac..."

"Jack," he stated, looking even more delicious not wearing his uniform.

"Whatcha got there in your shopping bag?"

"You're in a cheerful mood."

"I'm in a lot less pain, but the morning is still young."

"If it makes you feel any better, my body would be killing after a five-mile run," he said.

"My body is used to it. I exercise all the time."

"A health nut, huh? I'm not sure you'll like what I have in store for you this morning then."

"What is it?" I asked, trying to hide the worry in my voice.

"Sausages," he said, pulling a box of sausages out of the bag. "Bacon, eggs and pancake mix. More for me then?"

"Not a chance. Sounds delightful!"

"Oh and I got you this," he said, placing a black walkie talkie looking device on the counter.

"What is that? Some cop thing?"

"Kind of. It's a scanner. I know you'll be laid up for another day or two and you like those murder mystery shows so I figured you'd enjoy this too."

"What does it do?"

"You can listen to me while I'm at work."

"And why would I want to do that? It's like eavesdropping."

"People love these things, especially the elderly."

"Why, because they have nothing better to do?"

"Actually, yeah. If you don't like it I can just take it back," he said, clearly offended.

"It's great, thanks! Might be the oddest thing anyone has ever given me, though."

"It's just while you're sitting around. I'll take it back in a couple days."

"Okay. Now, onto breakfast," I said.

"Right. You sit and relax."

I planned on it.

I was all smiles watching Jack move around the kitchen making me breakfast. By the time he finished, my mouth was watering and my stomach grumbling. Jack seemed really sweet, which made me think his fiancé must be a complete idiot for letting him go.

"This is amazing," I gushed.

"Really?" Jack asked.

"Yes! You can cook for me every morning."

"Or for the next three weeks."

"Well, I have another job after this not too far from here or one that's out of state. The out of state is more money, but less time. I would like to ride out my summer here, but on the other hand I could get more money and hopefully find another housesitting job sooner. I'm so confused on what I should do."

"If you stay here, I'll cook you breakfast every morning," Jack said, winking at me.

"That's a major commitment. I am a huge bitch for a few days every month. Could you handle that?"

"I'd just take you out to breakfast."

"Oh no. I'm so irritable I don't even like being around anybody."

"Okay. I'd cook breakfast and leave it for you. You'd never have to see me."

I cracked up laughing. He wanted me to stay. This was the first time a guy had made me feel special since middle school. Well, besides my oldest brother of course.

"I'll think about it. It may just be the offer that keeps me here."

When we finished breakfast, Jack placed the leftover contents in the refrigerator and cleaned up the kitchen. I felt like I could watch him all day. I wondered if he knew how much I was drooling over his incredible body.

"Can I change your bandage for you?" he asked.

"Can I change your underwear?"

Jack looked at me completely puzzled and then burst out laughing.

"What? It's the same thing," I said.

"Not even close. I just want to make sure your foot is looking better. I mean, if you want to change my underwear, though..."

"I changed my bandage when I woke up. My foot is looking much better!"

"All right, well...I'll see you around."

What? He's leaving?

"Do you like board games?" I blurted out. Something inside me wanted him to stay.

"No."

"Card games?"

"Especially not."

I sat there on the bar stool, out of ideas on how to get him to keep me company while I was laid up. *What was I even doing right now?* I craved being solitary.

"I'll show you what I like to do when your foot is feeling better," he said, smirking.

"Tomorrow," I blurted.

"Tomorrow you will wake up and your foot will magically be all better?"

"I'm thinking so."

"Okay. Here's my number," he said, grabbing a piece of paper by the phone and jotting down his number with a pen. "Call or text me when your foot is healed. I have to work three to eleven today and tomorrow."

"Okay."

When Jack left, I tried to bust a dance move while hobbling on one foot and trying not to explode with excitement. I had never felt this way before. *I got his number! I got his number! But would I build up enough courage to use it?*

CHAPTER FOUR

The next morning my foot looked slightly better. Just as I was typing out a text to Jack, Jesse called.

"Hi!"

"Hey, are you still at Mrs. Penney's place?"

"I'm here right now."

"Awesome. They gave me the wrong coffee so now I have two and who better to share it with than my bestie?"

"Ooo! What kind?"

"Mocha!"

"Yes!" *My favorite.*

I was waiting for Jesse on the front steps when she arrived.

"Everything okay?" she asked, walking up the walkway.

"Yeah. It's nice out so I thought I would get some fresh air while I waited for you."

"Are you hiding something inside? Maybe a someone."

"No. I wish. Come in and see for yourself."

"I'm teasing. I know you would tell me all about it if you were."

"Well actually, there is this guy I just met."

"WHAT?" Jesse squealed.

"He's Mrs. Penney's nephew, but he's a police officer."

"Oh, that's not good. Well, what do you think?"

"That I wish I were normal because he's really nice."

"It's been awhile now, Clara Kate. Maybe just try."

"I'm damaged goods...nobody wants me."

"How old is he?"

"I never even thought to ask, but he knows I just graduated high school and he keeps coming around."

"Really?"

"Yeah. Well, he swims in the pool and goes in the hot tub, so technically he doesn't come here for me, but yesterday he made me breakfast."

"Doesn't come here for you my ass. He likes you! What's not to like?"

"My past," I grumbled, feeling deflated.

"Oh Clara Kate, all you can do is try. Okay?"

"All right."

We spent the day lounging by the pool. I listened to Jesse talk all about the different dates she had been on that week. Her date with Chad was a bust, but she wasn't looking to settle down anyway. She just wanted to enjoy her summer before college and have numerous one-night stands. I envied her.

"I have to go to work. I have to save every dollar I can for college, unlike some people," Jesse said, taking a jab at my plans to skip the college route and travel the world.

"Hey, you can come with me wherever I go."

"Yeah right, my parents would kill me. Your mother is going to murder you when she finds out your idea!"

"Goodbye," I said, pushing her towards the door.

"I love you."

"I love you, too."

I checked the time on my phone right when Jesse left. It was too late to text Jack now. I wanted to see him. Maybe I could spend the next few weeks pretending like I could have a normal relationship with him. If it didn't work, I could take the job in Texas and just leave. *What if Mrs. Penney wanted me to house sit again? I'd chance running into Jack. I better just leave well enough alone.*

I turned on the scanner for the first time. After a few minutes, I was bored and found it a little creepy listening in on other people's conversations. I guess I could see it was nice to know what was going on in your community, but who had the time to sit there and listen? I kept it on and went about my day.

As I was popping in my aerobics DVD, I heard a deep voice say my name over the scanner.

"I didn't get that. Repeat please," I heard the dispatcher say.

"Needed you to run a plate. All set, though," I heard Jack say. I grabbed my phone and sent him a text.

"Did you just say my name over the scanner?"

"Was wondering if you were listening. Now I know. Hi."

"Hi. Get back to work, taxpayer's dollars."

"You're not a taxpayer, so why do you care? You never texted me this morning."

"My friend stopped by with a coffee. Sorry."

"You have friends?"

"Goodbye, Jack Mac."

I didn't hear from Jack for the rest of the day. *I have friends? What a brat!* I was smiling from ear to ear thinking about Jack waiting for my text this morning. I think I was beginning to have a crush on him. It was way too soon to have these feelings. Maybe it was because he was the first guy to pay attention to me. He was really handsome, though and charming! *Ugh…*

****

I woke up to a text from Jack. He must have sent it the night before when he got off his shift, but I was sleeping.

"Can I take you out tomorrow?"

I wondered if I could text him back now or if it was too early. I decided to just go for it.

"I'd love that."

I got up and ate breakfast, wondering when I would hear from Jack. Then I showered and started to get ready. I was in my bra and underwear when I heard a knock on the door. I threw a shirt and some shorts on, running down the stairs to open the door.

"Good morning, Clara Kate."

"Jack."

"Getting ready for something?"

"Someone. He's tall, good looking and has a very deep masculine voice." *Oh my gosh...I can't believe I just told him that!*

"Do I?"

"Yes! It was intimidating at first, but now I like it."

"I see I'm growing on you."

DEFINITELY!

"Maybe," I said, smiling foolishly. "I have to run up and finish getting ready."

"You look great. Let's go."

"Blow dry hair...makeup," I turned to head up the stairs.

"Not where we are going. Come!" he said, grabbing the back of my oversized t-shirt and playfully tugging me back.

"Boo! You're no fun." I had never actually gotten ready for a guy...you know, looking nice and pretty. I was a little sad Jack didn't mind taking me out looking like a scrub. I locked up the house before hopping into his car and leaving.

"So, where are we going?"

"To have fun..."

"Okay Mr. Vague, doing what?"

"Hitting and riding."

I rolled my eyes at him, stifling my giggle. *What in the world does hitting and riding mean? Horseback riding? Do you hit a horse in order to ride him?* I had no idea. Moments later we pulled into a sports park called Sports Spread. This was definitely not a comfort zone for me. Jesse and I went to movies or shopping for clothes. I looked around, my eyes settling on a line of go karts.

"Is this place even open? It's dead here."

"It's a weekday. C'mon, you'll love it here!"

I highly doubt that!

"You ever try the batting cages?"

"Nope."

"Okay. Let's start on the slow speed," he said, getting out of his car and making his way down the cement walkway.

"How about no speed. I'll just watch you."

"That's no fun! Let's make a deal. If you hit more balls than I do, we can leave right now. Okay?"

"Fine."

"Grab a helmet over there," he said.

"Eww, it probably has bugs in it. I'm not wearing that!"

"Oh, you are such a baby! You're just afraid I'll beat you."

I went over to the rack of helmets and put one on. It was massive, shifting around on my head as I walked over to the cage.

"You can find a helmet that fits you," Jack called.

"All set."

"You can at least pretend like you're having fun."

"I'm having a blast!" I said sarcastically, as I scanned through the instructions and placed my coins in the machine. Twelve balls. All I had to do was hit twelve balls and I could leave this place.

"All right, both hands on the bat, elbow bent and up in the air...yes, just like that!"

Ugh, how annoying. The first ball came flying out as I jumped back. *Oh shit, that was fast*!

"Are you sure this is the slow?" I heard Jack laughing behind me. *Oh yeah, laugh it up*. I planted my feet firmly in place. I wasn't going to jump back this time.

"Eye on the ball. Keep your eye right on the ball," he coached.

Another ball came out and I took a swing at it and missed. *Damnit! This is harder than what I thought.*

"You're getting better. At least you swung that time."

Yeah...thanks. Errr! I can do this! Don't blink. Eyes. On. The. Prize. Another ball came out and I swung, connecting with it. The ball shot straight up and came down on my wrist. *Ow*!

"Shit, did that just hit you?"

"Yeah."

Jack opened the gate and came inside.

"Are you okay?" he asked, grabbing at my wrist, but I brushed him off.

"I'm fine...I'm counting that as one." Jack stepped behind me as another ball came out. I hit it, this time sending it forward into the mesh net. *Yes! Hole in one!* "Two," I sang. I missed all but two after that.

"What was that, eight?" he asked.

"Yes sir."

"That's awesome for your first try."

"And how many times have you done this?" I asked with a hint of attitude in my voice.

"I was here all the time growing up."

"Really? That's an unfair advantage. I didn't even know this place existed."

"Fine. I'll do the fast speed. Will that make it fair?"

"Oh yeah." I would love to see what fast speed was like after I just hit slow. I watched Jack walk over to the helmets and try a few on until he found one that fit. Then, he took a glove out of his back pocket and put it on. *Wow, he takes this stuff seriously.* He walked into the cage and inserted his coins. My eyes were fixed on his butt. The thought of already knowing what it looked like sent butterflies soaring through my heart. I liked his bum...a lot.

I hid my smile after he missed the first ball, but couldn't contain my laughter after the fourth.

"Laugh it up," he said, in between swings. He missed ball number five.

"Shit these are fast!" He hit the sixth and the seventh, but completely missed the eighth.

"Not even close, Jack."

"You want to try?"

"Hell no! It's intense just watching you. Do you give up yet?"

"Nope," he replied, hitting the ninth ball. That was his best hit yet. He missed the tenth and eleventh and then sent the final ball flying backwards. I jumped when it hit the fence.

"You win, let's go," he said, taking off his glove and helmet.

"No, that was fun. I don't want to do it again, but let's stay."

"Really?"

"Yeah." Jack grabbed my hand with a big smile and pulled me towards the go-karts. I stared at my fingers interlaced in his and almost tripped on a rock. Thankfully, Jack didn't notice. *Oh my gosh! I'm holding hands with him! My skin touching his skin. I have to tell Jesse!*

"Oh, hell no," I said, once I realized what Jack wanted me to do.

"What do you mean? I thought you wanted to stay."

"Nope. There is no way I am getting in one of those."

"Why? What are you so worried about?"

"Well, can I ride with you? There's two seats."

"There's also nobody else around. I'm not here to take some luxurious stroll around the track. I want to race!"

"No way!"

"Two cars?" the worker manning the go-karts asked.

"It's all him," I replied.

"C'mon, I'm not going by myself."

"They're perfectly safe. They only go up to twenty-five miles per hour. I mean, the only accidents I've ever seen is if two karts crash into each other, but our rule here is no bumping."

I looked from the man to Jack and then over to the go-karts again. *I guess the sparkly pink one did look pretty.* It was the only one in that color.

"How about I give you fifty bucks if you get into one of those karts and race me?" Jack asked.

"I'll match that fifty if you beat him," the man said.

Hmmm…a hundred bucks. I liked the sounds of that.

"Fine. Where are the helmets?"

"No helmets for this."

"Wait. You have to wear a helmet for baseball, but not for racing?"

"You'll see. It's not bad at all," the man said.

I made my way over to the pink sparkly kart and climbed inside. My heart instantly started racing. Jack must've been behind me because I couldn't see him.

"Seat belt on. Break here, gas here. When I wave the flag, that means go. Beat him, girl!" the attendant said, winking. *Easier said than done*! My foot was shaking on the pedal. Maybe this is what all my fellow classmates were doing while I sat at home watching television on Friday and Saturday nights.

The man waved the black and white checkered flag and I stepped my foot down hard on the gas, flying forward. *Jeez that's a loose pedal*. I backed my foot off slightly as I made my way around the track. I pictured myself skidding around the curves, but surprisingly the go-kart handled just fine. Halfway around I could see Jack out of the corner of my eye, but I was too afraid to look over.

"How are you doing?" he yelled.

"Fine," I lied.

"Good. Just wanted to make sure you were okay before I whooped your ass," he said, stepping on the pedal and passing me. *Whoop my ass? Hmmm…that sounds like a challenge. Let's see how fast this thing can go*! I stomped on the pedal once more when I got to the straight away. There was plenty of room to pass and I didn't think Jack would ever bump me if I attempted to beat him. Not only was I able to catch up to him, I blew right past him. I made two more laps, almost passing him again just before the man waved his flag for us to come in.

"You did something to her go-kart," Jack said, as I stood off to the side waiting.

"No sir! She won fair and square, although she did pick the fastest go-kart we own."

"What?"

"Yeah. No guy ever picks it because it's pink and glittery, so the girls are always winning," the man chuckled.

"Not fair."

"Is too," I said. "Pay up." The man reached into his wallet, but I shook my head at him. "No way, that was too much fun to get paid... from you anyway. You Jack can pay me my fifty dollars."

"Wow," he said, shaking his head and smiling. He reached into his wallet and pulled out two twenties and a ten-dollar bill.

"Thank you very much! Where to now? I have fifty dollars to spend!" Jack just shook his head again, thanking the man and walking off. I jogged a few steps, catching up to him.

"Are you mad at me? Here, I don't really want your money."

"Not at all. I just can't believe you beat me both times now and you don't even want to be here with me."

"Well when you put it that way...it sounds awful. I want to be here with you. I'm just not a sports girl."

"Could've fooled me."

"What's inside that building?" I asked, pointing to a tan metal building at the top of the hill.

"Arcade games."

"Oh, I've played those before. Let's go," I said, feeling rather brave and grabbing Jack's hand. If Jesse saw me right now she would freak! With my fingers intertwined with Jacks, I felt like the luckiest girl in the world.

We played arcade games for well over an hour. I forgot how much I loved Skee-Ball as a kid.

"That fifty bucks went quick!" I said, when we were all out of tokens.

"You want to see how many points we got? Maybe we'll get something cool from that prize redemption place over there," he said, pointing to a separate room.

"No. Maybe we'll come back here another day and add to our tickets."

"Okay. I love that idea!" he said. Just then my stomach started to rumble. "Can we hit a bucket of balls and then I'll take you out to lunch?"

"What does that even mean?" I asked, confused.

"Golf. You know, you get a club and some balls and hit them into an open field."

"What's the point of that?"

"Man, have you lived under a rock your entire life?"

I wish that were the case. I followed Jack to what was known as the driving range. I had never seen anything like it. Jack handed me a club and a bucket of balls. *Gosh, I'll be here all day.* I took my time practicing swinging and then I watched Jack hit a few. He didn't miss one golf ball the way he missed practically every baseball.

"Try it...you'll have fun."

I placed the ball down and swung my club as hard as I could, sending the ball flying into the field.

"Damn, wouldn't want to piss you off. Oh wait, I already have, multiple times."

"That was the old Clara Kate."

"So, there's a new Clara Kate?"

"Yes! And she's feeling adventurous," I said, playfully.

"How adventurous?"

"I don't know. Stick around and you'll find out," I replied, smiling at him.

"I plan on it."

Oh Lord, is this what flirting feels like?

"How old are you anyway?" I asked.

"Why? Does it matter?"

"I don't know. I'll be the judge of that after you tell me your age."

"How old do you want me to be?"

"My best friend has this rule about twice her age and since we're eighteen she says anyone under thirty-six is okay, but I beg to differ."

"Oh yeah?"

"Yeah. I think twenty-five would be my cut off."

Jack laughed.

"Why twenty-five?"

"I don't know. It just seems like a nice number, although I'm not really into odd numbers. Let's go with twenty-four instead."

"Or twenty-six."

I stopped and looked at Jack, afraid to ask if he was twenty-six.

"Don't look at me like that. Age doesn't matter, Clara Kate. When you like somebody then that's all that matters, right?"

HE LIKES ME?

"Maybe..." I replied.

"I'm twenty-four by the way, which means I made your so called cut off. You can relax now," he said, after he watched me hit a few more balls. *Phew! I could work with twenty-four. Ugh...what was I saying? I'm not sure I could work with anything.*

After we each finished hitting an entire bucket of balls, we left the sports complex in search of some lunch. We ended up at this hole in the wall pizza shop.

"Before I forget, thank you for today," I said.

"Do you really mean that?"

"Yes. I was definitely uncomfortable at times, but overall, I really enjoyed myself."

"Good."

I ordered a salad and some buffalo tenders. Jack ordered a pepperoni pizza. He offered to pay for mine, but it didn't feel right, given the fact that he had just given me fifty dollars.

"If you share your pizza, I'll share my chicken and salad."

"Deal," he said, reaching out his hand. I took it and shook it. *Oh, I loved his big strong hand.*

When my number was called, I took my order to a corner booth and sat down. Jack followed behind me.

"Here, have some while you wait for yours," I said. Jack was happy to oblige.

A few moments later his number was called. I watched him walk to get his order. I was with the hottest guy in this entire establishment.

"Hey Jack! Long time no see," the kid behind the counter said to Jack. They exchanged a handshake. "So, Scotty and Jezebel now, huh?"

"Yeah? Where'd you hear that?"

"They came in the other night for some pizza looking awfully friendly."

"They've always been close."

"Oh yeah, I'd definitely say holding hands and kissing is close."

I watched Jack drop the pizza on the counter and walk out of the restaurant. I snatched my purse, leaving my food behind and bolted after him.

"Jack. Where are you going?"

"Screw this pizza place!" he barked, his whole demeanor changing.

"Okay. We can go somewhere else..."

"No. I need to talk to Scotty."

"Who is Scotty and who's Jezebel?"

"Get in the car, we're leaving," he demanded, hopping into the driver's side of his car. I quickly opened the passenger side and got in.

"You're acting a little crazy right now. We paid for food and now we're just going to leave it?"

"If you're so hungry then why don't you just stay and eat?"

"WHAT IS GOING ON RIGHT NOW?" I asked, raising my voice. Jack stopped at a red light and punched his steering wheel. "What did that kid say to you?"

"My fiancé and my fucking best friend are now fucking!"

"What? Screw them. Screw the both of them! Who gives a shit?"

"She's a liar and so is he! Telling me she wants to travel more. Yeah, across town to my best friend's bed!"

"Okay, do you even know if that's the truth?"

"God damnit. That mother fucker was my best friend since elementary school!"

"I'm not going with you. Drop me off. This is absolutely ridiculous! So, what, you're going to go over there and do what?"

"Knock his fucking teeth out! I hope she's there too, to watch me beat the shit out of him."

"Okay, woah! Easy! Nobody is beating the shit out of anybody. You need to calm down."

"Don't tell me to calm down. You have no fucking clue how I'm feeling right now. My entire world was turned upside down a few weeks ago and it was that asshole who did it! I should've been on my honeymoon by now! I should be climbing into bed every night holding my wife...BUT I'M NOT!"

Oh no. This isn't good! What should I do? He can't go beat someone up! He's a cop, for goodness sakes! Could he get fired? Think...Think...THINK!

Jack pulled into Mrs. Penney's driveway and waited for me to get out.

"Are you getting out?" he asked, after I was clearly still sitting there in his passenger seat. I didn't want to move. I was terrified of what Jack was about to go do.

"I was raped," I blurted out, with my hands on my knees staring out the passenger side window. *Oh. My. Gosh! Did I really just tell this man I've been raped?*

"What?" he asked instantly, but I knew he heard exactly what I said.

"When I was fourteen, at a campground I was staying at one summer with my best friend and her family." I couldn't believe I was telling Jack *my* story.

"Oh my..." he began, but I cut him off.

"For some reason the mosquitos love me and when I get bit by one, the bite swells up huge, so that night I doused myself in bug spray. We went fishing down by the pond that the campground owned; they stocked it themselves. We were getting nibbles here and there, but the fish weren't that big yet.

We decided to go back to our cabin. I wanted to wash all the bug spray off before I climbed into bed, so I went to the communal bathroom by myself to take a shower. I was almost finished when the shower curtain opened and I saw this police officer. I didn't really have time to look at him, but he had this jet-black mustache. He was clean shaven everywhere else.

He slammed my face against the bathroom wall," I said, my voice failing me. Jack grabbed my hands and rubbed his thumbs over my fingers. "It hurt so bad. I remember wondering how long it was going to go on for. It wasn't long and he never spoke. He left when he was done. I slid down the shower stall and just cried. There was blood coming out of me and flowing down the drain."

I started crying. I had never told a single person the details from that night. I thought that if I had blocked it all out then it would just go away. It's been four years and it hasn't worked. The psychiatrist my mother sent me to told me over and over again that I needed to talk about whatever it was that happened to me. *Maybe once it's all out, I can move on and start having a functional relationship with a guy like Jack.*

"I don't know how long I sat there and cried. A mother and her young daughter found me. The mother was in shock. She shut the shower off, grabbed a towel and wrapped it around me. When she questioned me, I told her I just got my period for the first time and was freaking out because I didn't know what to do. I asked her if I would bleed out or if it would eventually stop. She bought the whole story."

"Why? Why did you lie? They could've taken you to the hospital and done a rape kit on you."

"I don't know. It seemed easier to lie. He was a police officer, so I thought they would never find him."

"That's not true!"

"I asked the lady to walk me back to my cabin. I was shaking so badly that she had to dress me. They did. They walked me back. I felt enormous relief when I was back with Jesse and her family, like I was safe again. The woman had told Jesse's family I wasn't feeling well, most likely because her father was right there and she didn't want to tell him about my period fiasco. When the woman left, I told Jesse's family I felt very sick. They were all kinds of freaking out, telling me I looked as white as a ghost and I was shaking uncontrollably. Her mom ran to the convenience store and bought a thermometer, but obviously I didn't have a fever."

"I don't get it. You couldn't confide in your best friend? I mean, they would've helped you."

"It was my secret; it still is." I looked into Jack's eyes knowing full well he didn't agree with me. I turned away and continued looking out the car window as I finished my story.

"My mother came and picked me up. It was a two-hour drive. I was relieved when I was finally on my way home. I trembled that entire two hours with Jesse's family, so they were in my face asking all these questions, but when my mom came, the trembling stopped. It was weird."

"Your body was probably in hyper mode being right where you were raped and knowing your mom was bringing you far away to safety..."

"Not far enough away. I started having flashbacks and these panic attacks. Well, at first, I didn't know what was happening. The first time was in the bathroom after I turned the water on. My chest hurt and I couldn't breathe. I thought I was having a heart attack. Then I figured my mind would turn off at night while I slept, but it became torturous to sleep with all the nightmares, so I started experiencing insomnia. I would stay up eating all night and was a zombie at school the next day. I gained at least fifty pounds."

"And your mother never questioned you?"

"She did, but I never told her. She thought I was being bullied at school. She questioned Jesse. After a few months and Jesse threatening to never talk to me again, I broke down and told her, but in minimal detail. She was in shock and wanted to go to the police, but I made her swear to secrecy."

"And she did?"

"I don't think so. In fact, I think she told a lot of people. I mean, everyone acted different around me...her parents and our friends at school. Maybe I was just paranoid, but no guy ever even tried to approach me. Even when I forced myself to go to the school dances with friends, no guy would ever ask me to dance."

"And if they did?"

"No way. I'd shut them right down. I didn't even want to be touched by Jesse, let alone a guy who had a penis who could potentially rape me."

"Jeez, Clara Kate."

"I know," I said. I was well aware of how broken inside I was. "My mother sent me to a therapist after the weight gain and my grades slipping. I wouldn't talk to her either."

"Why? I don't get it. He's out there probably doing it to another girl at some other campground."

"I want to pretend it never happened."

"How is that working out for you?"

"Clearly it's not. That night I first saw you, I was frozen. My feet with broken shards of glass sending this heinous pain up my leg and I couldn't move. I thought it was going to happen all over again."

"Clara Kate, I would never do anything to hurt you," he said, wrapping his arm around me and leaning his head into the crook of my neck. "I'm so sorry."

"Please don't say that."

"But I am. I wish I could undo your past and take it all away."

"Me too," I choked.

"I promise you will never see me in my uniform again," he said, looking into my empty deep blue eyes.

"I don't know. Maybe it's good that I do. It didn't trigger any flashbacks like when it first happened. I couldn't even look at our school resource officer for a while. Ugh, no way! I even had to take sponge baths for almost a year. Any running water made me feel so incredibly uncomfortable. I've come a long way on my own."

"You're so skinny now. How did you manage to lose all the weight?"

"My mom. My junior year of high school I started house sitting, first with your aunt and then through word of mouth, it just took off. The only way my mom would let me house sit during school was if I exercised and kept my grades up. There was something about house sitting that was exhilarating. I knew at any moment some guy could come knock on the door and hurt me, but I was going to fight back this time. I wasn't going to let it happen again. Each time I house sat I was proving to myself that I could be outside of my safety net, away from Jesse and my family. It gave me confidence. So, for that reason alone I really wanted to house sit. I bought this work out video and did it every night. At first I hated exercising, but that's when I would let all my negative thoughts from that day just drain right out of me."

"You must've felt so alone."

"I enjoy being alone, which hurts, because Jesse and I were inseparable. It affected every square inch of my entire world."

"And now?"

"I shower...no more sponge baths. One day I threw away the hand sanitizer and started washing my hands again at the sink like a normal person. I think this is as good as it's going to get."

"And if I want you to let me in?"

"I am letting you in. I'm pouring my entire heart out to you right now."

"What if I want more?"

"Not even your light could shine bright enough for my shade of darkness."

"I don't get it. Why are you telling me all of this then?"

"I want you to stay with me right now because I enjoy being around you," I confessed. "Besides, I don't want you to go find your ex-fiancé and beat the crap out of your best friend...or ex-best friend now. You don't need that kind of trouble."

"So you thought that by telling me your story that I would no longer leave?"

"Yes. Did it work?"

Jack cracked a slight smile.

"Definitely."

"Okay then. Let's go inside."

We sat down on the couch, my stomach rumbling with hunger.

"You still hungry?" he asked.

"Yes, but that's okay."

"I'm sorry I was so short with you back there at the pizza place. I'll go make us something to eat."

"We could go back and see if our food is still there now that you've calmed down," I said, smiling innocently.

"Not a chance. I'll see what my aunt has," he said, his smile matching mine. "Thank you for telling me your story," he said, kissing me on the cheek. "Is that okay?"

"Kissing me?"

"Yeah. I don't want to make you feel uncomfortable."

"That night I told you about Madeline and you held me, it felt so good. It was just for a minute, but in that minute, I wondered if I would be able to feel an emotional attachment with a guy...more specifically, you."

"And?"

"I don't know."

"So if I held your hand?" he asked, taking my hand in his.

"I like that."

"And if I put my arm around you like this?" he asked, sliding closer to me on the couch and reaching his arm around my neck.

"Oh gosh. I feel like I'm in middle school right now. The years where heavy petting was fulfilling." Jack cracked up laughing. When he was finished, he turned and looked at me.

"What?" I asked.

"Just looking at you..."

"I bet you look at me a lot differently now."

"I do. I thought you were this selfish stuck up bitch who didn't have any friends because you weren't worth getting to know. Now I think you are incredibly brave and fearless. You're a reminder not to judge a book by its cover."

"If you thought I was this awful person, then why do you keep coming around?"

"My ego isn't afraid of you. My first attempt at a family, my son dies. My second attempt, I'm left at the altar. There isn't anything you could say or do that hasn't been done before." With that, Jack got up off the couch and wandered into the kitchen.

But this hasn't been done before. I was raped. I am ruined. Although the truth was, I felt this weight lifted off my shoulders now. My big secret was out. I think I just had my first real breakthrough. Okay, not my first, but my first in years! Deep down, I knew I wanted to be a part of whatever Jack was, although I wasn't sure I could ever give him what he wanted. I was afraid I wasn't actually capable of being his girl.

Jack found some frozen pizza in the freezer and cooked it in the oven.

"Not as good as the pizza place," he mumbled, in between bites.

"Maybe if you weren't so hot-headed."

"I know. That kid just irritated me. He was a freshman when I was a senior and he was such a shit stirrer in school. Apparently he still is."

"You need to learn the art of ignoring. Maybe Jezebel is dating Scotty, which is really mean and hurtful, but what positivity are you getting out of hurting Scotty? You want to lower yourself to their level to be mean and hurtful just like them? You're better than that!"

I was trying to be genuine and here Jack was, smiling at me. He dropped his pizza crust on the plate, wiping the crumbs off his fingers with a napkin and told me he had to leave. I was still afraid I wasn't getting through to him.

"Bye," he said.

"Seriously. Fly high," I said, wrapping my arms around him and giving him a hug. He was just as surprised as I was by my own gesture.

"Okay."

"You will? No going over there!" I wasn't sure why I felt this need to protect him.

"I get it, fly high. I'll see you tomorrow."

"I will?"

"You will."

CHAPTER FIVE

I woke up to the doorbell ringing. I checked the time, just before eight o'clock. A smile spread across my face picturing Jack at the door. I quickly brushed my teeth and ran down the stairs, opening the door to find Jesse standing there, crying on the front step. Her black mascara was running down her cheeks.

"Jesse. Are you okay? What happened?"

"I just got kicked out."

"Oh my gosh. Your mother kicked you out? What did you do?" I pulled her inside and sat her on the couch, grabbing a tissue and wiping at her eyes.

"No. I really liked him."

"Chad?"

"No, this other guy. You should've seen the look on his face when he rolled over and realized I was still there. He called me a cab. He didn't say a word, Clara Kate. He literally rolled back over, picked up his phone and started telling the cab company his address."

"Seriously? What did you do?"

"I felt like a total idiot. I told him, 'I own a fucking car you moron, don't ever call me again,' but I really liked him and wish so bad he would call me which he probably never will because I started crying right then and there."

"Oh Jesse. I'm so sorry. He sounds like a total jerk!"

"Ugh, why can't I ever just find a good one?"

"Oh, listen to you. Just the other day you were telling me you just wanted to date all summer, nothing serious."

"I know. I just thought he was the one."

"How long had it been?"

"A few dates."

"Are you hearing yourself right now?" I laughed. I scolded myself inwardly for laughing at Jesse. Here I was, all goo goo ga ga for Jack, ready to push myself out of my comfort zone, when I've only known him for just about a week. "Sorry," I said. "It's just...you're going off to college, so it wouldn't make sense to find the love of your life right now. Okay? You have the rest of your life and an entire sea of fish. You are beyond beautiful...you'll find the one!"

"I know. That's why I came here. I needed to hear your negative outlook on relationships."

"I don't have a negative opinion on relationships..."

"Sure you do! You get grossed out when a guy even checks you out. It's like you're a lesbian."

"I was raped, Jesse! You have no idea what that's like! Every fucking guy that looks at me...all I think about is if they're going to rape me. Do you honestly think I want to be this dysfunctional?"

Just then there was a knock at the door. I angrily swung it open, finding Jack standing there with a coffee in one hand and a small white paper bag in the other.

"You okay?" he asked, before I realized I had forgotten to hide my irritation with Jesse.

"Yeah. My friend is here right now. Can I call you later?" I asked. Just then Jesse was by my side.

"Hi! I'm Jesse."

"The best friend. Hi, I'm Jack."

"I've heard all about you," she said, smiling at him. *Oh, there she goes again with that look in her eyes*. I watched her literally eye-fucking Jack as he stood there.

"Okay, well I'll leave you two ladies alone. I brought you a coffee and a bagel. I hope you enjoy," he said, handing me the coffee and bag.

"Come on in. We were just talking," Jesse purred.

"Ah, that's okay," he said, turning to leave.

"C'mon, I don't bite," she giggled. *Those tears dried up quick!*

"But she humps," I whispered to myself. *Errr*! I smiled at Jack, letting him know it was okay to come in. In fact, I think it was best so that I didn't choke Jesse out.

"Okay," Jack said, turning to come inside. "Did you check the baskets in the pool or add any chemicals today?"

"Not yet."

"I'll do it for you," he said, walking through the living room and into the backyard.

"Holy muscles and those eyes, Clara Kate! How the hell did you snag a guy like that?"

"Oh, thanks a lot."

"I didn't mean it like that. I mean, I know how you snagged him. You're gorgeous, Clara Kate, but how the hell have you kept him? Guys only want one thing."

"He hasn't wanted it yet."

"Seriously? Has he tried to kiss you?"

"No."

"That's odd. Maybe he's gay."

"Nope. I told him."

"About what happened?"

"I told him everything."

"Wow! And he's still coming around?"

"I know. I'm freaking out. Part of me was hoping the idea of me being raped would push him away, but the other part really wants him to stay. I'm so confused. What should I do? I think I'm leading him on."

"Clara Kate! Go for it!"

"You mean...sex?"

"Yes! Make sure he wears a condom since you aren't on birth control. You don't want to get pregnant."

"I don't think I can do it. What if he inserts his penis inside of me and I have a flashback?"

"What if he's inside of you and you don't have a flashback?"

"Uggghhhh...I don't know what to do!" I cried in frustration. "What if we have sex and it hurts and I cry?"

"It might hurt. It hurt me the first few times. It's supposed to. The walls of your vagina are expanding."

"Will I bleed again?"

"Maybe...I didn't."

"No. I don't think I'm ready."

"I can take him off your hands," she sang cheerfully and winked at me.

"Oh shut up! You better never do that to me. I really like him. He has a lot of baggage, but he's really sweet."

"What kind of baggage?"

"He lost a child and his fiancé called off their wedding."

"Oh wow. It sounds like he has just as bad of trust issues as you."

"A match made in heaven," I joked.

"Just kiss him and see where that leads."

"I know where it will lead."

"Well just tell him you want to take it slow. If he likes you, he will listen. I'd say he really likes you, though because he's outside right now doing the chores you're being paid for."

I looked outside to see him emptying the basket for the pool. It was my least favorite chore to do every time I watched Mrs. Penney's house. I lifted up that cover every morning never knowing what I was going to find. Half the time I found a dead mouse or a drowned frog.

"I'm going to run upstairs and get dressed. I'll be right back," I said, heading up the stairs to change out of my pajamas. When I returned back downstairs, I found Jesse and Jack outside sitting at the patio table.

"Well, I'll leave you two love birds alone," Jesse said, getting up to leave. I shot her a venomous look. *Love birds? Seriously Jesse?*

"Love birds, huh?" Jack asked after Jesse left.

"Don't mind her. She's clinically insane. The doctors have actually diagnosed her as crazy!"

"I don't buy that for one minute. What were you two ladies talking about while I was out here?"

"Mums the word."

"She's awfully friendly."

"She's available if you'd like to take her out on a date. She thought you were super good looking and she loves having sex." *Why was I saying this? Er! Because I need to know if he liked what he saw.*

"I'm not here for her."

"No?" I asked, grinning from ear to ear. Jack shook his head.

"Tell me how Jamison died."

Jack took a deep breath and exhaled before answering.

"He drowned in my parent's swimming pool. He was in my mother's care at the time and she had put him down for a nap. He somehow got out of his room, opened the back slider and wandered into the pool. Why do you ask?"

Wow! I swallowed the lump in my throat.

"I've told you everything. I just want to feel like you will tell me everything too."

"So I can gain your trust?"

"Maybe. This is all new to me."

"I'll do whatever it takes."

"But what if that's not enough?" I asked, holding back my tears.

"I don't have any set goals for you and me. Hell, I just got out of a committed relationship, so let's just say I'm not ready to bring you home to mom and dad. I like spending time with you. There are no strings attached here. All right?"

"Okay."

"Besides, are you even sticking around here?"

"No. I'm going to house sit internationally after this summer. There are a ton of people in...say Europe, that will pay a good amount of money for you to stay at their home. You should see these places. It'll be like a dream come true. I will get to meet all these people!"

"You're not afraid to travel alone?"

"Oh I am! Deathly afraid actually. If I don't push myself to go outside my comfort zone, though, then I will be a slave to Missouri my entire life. My mom was born here, grew up here and will probably die here too. I don't want that. I just want to float through the air and go where the wind takes me."

"That actually sounds pretty amazing."

"Thanks. I haven't told anybody yet. Well, just you and Jesse."

"Do you think your mom will be okay with it?"

"Heck no. She shoved college applications in my face before my junior year was even over."

"So what'd you do?"

"Applied to every one she gave me."

"Didn't that cost money?"

"Yeah, but having money to pay for college applications was never an issue. I did literally nothing in high school for fun, Jack. I saved just about every penny I earned from house sitting. All the money I would get from my birthday and the holidays would pay for all the things Jesse and I did. In fact, I usually paid for Jesse too. Her parents don't have a lot of money."

"Can I ask you something?" Jack asked.

"Yeah."

"Have you ever kissed a guy?"

"Yeah. Well, a few, but they were boys...in middle school. After what happened, though, no...never."

Jack nodded his head.

"It's too much for you. I totally get it. That's why I've never applied myself even when I thought a guy was cute. I've completely accepted the fact that this rape has made me an intimacy degenerate and I may be alone for the rest of my life."

"Don't say that."

"Who else out there in this world can say they've never kissed a guy by the age of eighteen? It's not normal!"

"You had something taken from you that wasn't there to take. Your intimacy, your virginity and your choice as to who the first guy would be to share those things with."

"I think that was the worst part. It was my virginity. It was my say in who I gave it to. It was something so incredibly special to me. I watch Jesse running around sleeping with a new guy every other night, thinking how clueless she is...knowing that she has no idea how special intimacy is. I know, though because it's something I so badly want to have, but so afraid to give," I cried.

Jack got out of his chair and came over to mine. He scooped me up into his arms and then sat in my chair holding me. He wrapped his arms around me and kissed me on the head. *Gosh I loved being in his arms*. Right then and there I closed my eyes and thanked God for putting me in these two strong arms that made me feel so unbelievably safe.

CHAPTER SIX

I woke in the morning feeling quite refreshed, like a whole new woman. I still couldn't believe how honest I had been with Jack these past few days. Part of me was proud of myself and the other part was just filled with pure fear. I wondered how advanced he was. I mean, he obviously has had sex since he had a child. I tried to brush the insecurities of knowing my intimacy delays out of my mind. I was never going to get where I so badly wanted to be if I constantly dwelled on how immature I was.

It wasn't just that. I didn't understand why Jack would want someone six years younger. Maybe he really did only want what Jesse said all guys wanted and I was just a safe bet since I had plans to leave. I hopped out of bed, literally shaking off my negative vibes. *Today was going to be a good day.*

After I ate breakfast, showered and did my daily chores, I decided it was a good day for cooking. I didn't cook. In fact, I only remember cooking once when I made brownies for a bake sale in middle school. I always wanted to see what it was like to move around the kitchen with confidence. Growing up, I'd sit at the barstool and watch my mother cook. I never did dare to ask if I could help because she moved so quickly, I'd surely be getting in her way.

I took my phone, typing homemade brownies into the google search engine and finding a five-star recipe. It took more time finding all the ingredients in Mrs. Penney's kitchen than actually preparing the batter. When I turned to place them in the oven, I realized I had never preheated it. *Right. That would've helped.*

I sat on the barstool waiting for the oven to preheat. *What would I make next? Cookies*! I was bursting with this new-found energy inside my soul. I smiled to myself as I went about the kitchen searching for the ingredients. I had everything, including exactly two eggs left. The brownies were still baking as I scooped balls of cookie dough onto two baking sheets. I sat on the stool again and grabbed my phone, noticing I had received a text from Jack fifteen minutes ago.

"Good morning, beautiful."

I took my phone off vibrate mode.

"Morning."

I wondered if there would be a knock at my door any minute. I never knew what time of day I'd be seeing Jack, although it was never between three and eleven since that was his shift at work. That was the perfect shift to maximize the day.

Just then the timer went off. I took the brownies out, inserting a toothpick in the middle which came out clean. *Nice*! I turned the oven up twenty-five degrees, waiting a few minutes for it to beep telling me it was ready and then slid the cookie sheets in. I snapped a picture and sent it to Jack.

"Are you going to help me eat some of these?" I typed out underneath the picture.

"Wow. Those look amazing. You're sexy and you bake. You're quite the catch!"

Ha! I wish. I didn't text anything back. I switched the cookie sheets around halfway through their baking time, then sat there waiting for the timer to beep. When it did, I waited for the cookies to cool down before placing them on the cooling rack. *I was rocking this whole baker thing!*

I texted my brother to use the car.

"What do you need it for?" he texted back right away.

"I'm house sitting at Mrs. Penney's house and I need to go to the grocery store to buy food." When he didn't text right back again, I knew I wasn't getting the car. *Ugh, he was so annoying, dictating when and where I can drive the car mom said we were supposed to SHARE!*

"I'm still laying in bed. I'll drop you off at the store in a few hours."

What? Asshole!

"Just forget it," I said and never heard back. I hated my life here and couldn't wait to move far away where I could buy my own vehicle and not rely on anyone else but myself.

After I was done baking, I decided to walk to the store. I chuckled to myself, knowing the last time I made this walk was to buy a lock to keep Jack out of the backyard. *How did that work out for me? Not too well...*

When I arrived at the store, I had to be picky with what I bought since I would have to carry it for a mile back home. I didn't need much anyway; I'd only be staying at Mrs. Penney's for one more week. I decided to take the house-sitting job here in Missouri. It was just down the road. I wasn't ready for a big move like Texas, especially since I wanted to see where Jack and I were going. If I moved now, I'd definitely miss him and always wonder what might've been. I think I'll tell him the next time I see him.

A few Lean Cuisines and a couple one skillet frozen meals later, I was headed back home. Of course Mrs. Penney told me I could eat any food in her house, but I had done a bang-up job on both her refrigerator and freezer. I didn't want her to come back home to an empty house.

Right as the driveway came into view, I could see my brother driving in our car. He pulled into the driveway and beeped.

"I'm right here," I said, stopping at his window. "You said a few hours."

"It hasn't even been a few hours."

"Well forget it, I already went. Thanks anyway."

"You're so impatient. I would've driven you so don't go running to mom crying."

"Whatever," I said, walking away. Just the sight of him pissed me off. I don't even think he had a job, so I'm not sure what he needed the car for. *Was he always going to be this self-absorbed asshole?* We hardly ever got along. Thank God I had my other brother! He was compassionate and considerate...he'd do anything for me. I didn't understand how two of my brothers from the same mother and father born two years apart could be so different.

I heard my brother back down the driveway as I unlocked the door. I made my way inside and microwaved myself some lunch! *Yum.* Ever since I met Jack, I no longer want to be alone. He consumes every thought in my mind. It wasn't just that, though. He made me want to get out and go do stuff. Before Jack, I was perfectly content with sitting around, but now as I sit here pigging out on my brownies and cookies, I just want to go explore. I could easily be happy taking another walk to the grocery store, whereas before I saw it as a dreaded chore. Maybe I was maturing or working through my pain, but either way, I knew Jack had something to do with it.

Just then I heard the door open. I hopped off the stool to find Jack walking across the living room.

"Don't you knock?"

"Don't you lock?"

"Very funny."

"Honey, I'm home," he called.

"I was just in here, eating the fruits of my labor," I said, making my way back into the kitchen.

"Wow. You couldn't even wait for me?"

"I was just taste testing to see if they were any good," I laughed.

"Oh, I see how it is. I'll be the judge of that," he said, taking one cookie and one brownie. "So good, but now I need some milk," he said, getting off the bar stool.

"Sit. I'll get it."

"You're the best!"

"If you keep telling me that I might believe it."

"Good. Because you are!"

"What's that?" I asked, glancing at a white shiny piece of paper on the counter.

"Actually, that's what I came here to talk to you about." The smile disappeared from his face. *Uh-oh.*

"What is it?" I asked.

"Well, I talked to Jesse...you know...when we were outside together on the patio the other day. She told me the town of the campground you were assaulted in and so I did some investigating. I think the man who raped you was just pretending to be a cop and he's in jail now."

"Wait...what? You talked to Jesse about my rape?" I had told Jack way more about my rape than Jesse because it was a safe move. I hardly knew Jack. Jesse...it was all too personal to tell Jesse.

"You're upset about that? I mean, you told her my fiancé left me and about my son's death. Both of those things are very personal, yet you tell someone who is a complete stranger to me."

Shit! Jesse has a big mouth!

"So what does that mean? Now we're even?"

"No. That's not what this is about! I spent all last night and all today trying to find the man that raped you and I think I found him. Is this him?" he asked, picking the piece of paper up off the counter and flipping it over. He brought it closer to my face. My chest started getting tighter. My head felt warm and the rest of my body cold. My world started to close in on me, a dark black cloud around my vision. The last thing I remember Jack telling me was that the man was a serial rapist.

When I awoke, there was another police officer, an EMT and a paramedic.

"Clara Kate, can you hear me?"

I kept blinking my eyes, wondering where the hell I was.

"Yes."

"Okay. We're going to try and sit you up. Do you feel okay?"

"No. What is happening to me?"

"It seems as though you may have blacked out. Is this a regular occurrence?"

I shook my head.

"Your friend Jack is here with us and his partner."

Partner? He's gay? Oh right, the other police officer.

"We're going to take your blood pressure again in a few minutes. It's dangerously low right now so you might have to come with us to the hospital."

Jack's face came into view as he knelt down beside me. I remember what happened now. The man...the man who raped me...Jack found him.

"I'm so sorry," he said, stroking my cheek.

"What the hell are you doing?" I growled.

"What do you mean?" he asked, a confused look on his face.

I tried to sit up, the paramedic helping me as I turned to face Jack.

"What makes you think I want to see that man's face?"

"I don't know. I thought that if I tried to find him then he couldn't hurt anyone else and if it was this guy," he said, shaking the picture, "then you would be happy to know he is behind bars."

"Don't...don't show me that picture again!"

"Gone," he said, crumpling it up and heading towards the trash.

"No! Don't do that. Don't throw that away here. Get it out!"

"Okay...alright. I'm sorry."

"You had no right doing that! This is my story! I told you things I never told ANYBODY! You took my words and you used them to hurt me just like everybody else!"

"I was trying to help you. Don't you see that?"

"NO! I DON'T SEE THAT! YOU'VE MADE MY LIFE WORSE! I'VE TRIED FOR YEARS TO GET THE IMAGE OF THAT FACE OUT OF MY

FUCKING HEAD. DON'T YOU GET THAT? NOW I'LL BE MESSED UP ALL OVER AGAIN."

I brushed the paramedic off and stood up. I instantly felt lightheaded again, bending over and placing my hands on my knees. I lifted my head to look at Jack again.

"If you want to help me then leave and don't come back."

"You don't mean that. You're just upset right now. I get it," he said, coming closer to me.

"NO! I trusted you..."

"Let's go," his partner suggested.

"I can't believe you're doing this right now," Jack said.

"I can't believe you would go behind MY back and talk to Jesse about what happened and then turn it into some investigating journey just to fill some cop happy desire within WITHOUT ever asking me if that's what I wanted. You only thought about you then, so keep thinking about you now and forget about me."

Jack shook his head.

"Go! Goodbye! Don't ever come back here..." I seethed through gritted teeth.

"He won't come back here," his partner said, placing his hand on Jack's shoulder. I put my head down. I couldn't look at Jack anymore. I was disgusted with him. I heard the door close and sunk back down onto the floor crying.

"I'm sorry, miss. Are we able to take your blood pressure again?"

"Sure," I replied. The paramedic snickered, telling me my numbers before were dangerously low and now they were too high.

"I'm fine...really. Jack just showed me a picture of a man who attacked me four years ago. I think I had a panic attack. Can you pass out from a panic attack?"

"You didn't just pass out. We took at least five minutes getting here and Jack said you laid there with your eyes closed the entire time. He thought you were dead."

"Good. Serves him right! Jerk..."

"Just take a few breaths in and exhale. Don't think about any of that right now. I want to make sure you are okay before we leave."

"Don't think about it? Yeah right! That's all I'll probably think about for the rest of my life," I laughed sarcastically. "I can't believe that guy. Who the hell does he think he is? And just when I started thinking I was going to be okay."

"Some people do things and they can't see past their end goal in order to think about how others might feel. I don't know him and I don't know you, but in the end, you have to ask yourself if the relationship you two have is worth ending or can it be fixed? Can there be forgiveness? You know, back in the old days, forgiveness wasn't an option; it was a given. That's what the bible preaches too. Nowadays, forgiveness depends on how much you love someone."

Who the hell was this guy? A priest?

"Wow. That was a really good speech, Fred," the EMT said to the paramedic.

"Thanks. You know where I heard that?"

"No. Where?"

"At a funeral service last week. The pastor told us that forgiveness was a requirement back in the day and not a choice. It got me wondering what life would be like if everyone still practiced that."

I sat there wondering what it would be like if I was able to forgive everyone who had wronged me. I wasn't sure that was even possible.

"Well, I'd say I've calmed down enough. Would you like to take my blood pressure one last time?"

"Well, since you twisted my arm," he said. I smiled and offered him my arm.

"Perfect. I think our work here is done," the paramedic said before the EMT started packing up.

"Well, sorry you guys had to come out here and see me get ugly. I really am a nice person." They both chuckled before leaving Mrs. Penney's house. *Ahhh...peace at last.*

What the hell just happened? This morning I woke up pretending like I could play a housewife for Jack, baking it up in the kitchen as my thoughts ran wild and now I never wanted to see him again. *What in the world was he thinking? Why would he think I'd even care where that evil varmint of a human being ended up?* What a complete and utter idiot! And what about Jesse, talking about the death of his son. *Who did she think she was?* I called her right away.

"Hello?" she answered.

"Are you busy?"

"I'm at work, but what's up?"

"What did you say to Jack about his fiancé leaving him and the death of his son?"

"Nothing...just what you told me."

"Which was?"

"I don't know. I went outside and started talking to him."

"What did you say to him? I want to know exactly word for word."

"I don't remember. What is all this about? Did you two get into an argument?"

"Jesse! Why would you talk to him about such personal things from his past?"

"I have no idea. I walked outside and said 'hey' and then we had absolutely nothing to talk about, so I just apologized for his fiancé leaving him and losing a child. I don't see the harm in that."

"Did it ever occur to you that maybe he doesn't want you, a complete stranger to him, knowing such intimate things?"

"I guess, but he asked about your rape."

"Yeah, I know. The sad part is that you actually entertained his questions."

"What? Now I'm the bad guy? I did nothing wrong here! Don't blame me for the fact that you two got into a fight."

"Really? Because you are the exact reason I just kicked him out and told him never to come back. If it wasn't for you, he would have never known where to find a guy that goes around raping girls in a fake police officer uniform," I growled, hanging up in her face and slamming my phone down on the counter. "AHHH!" I yelled.

My phone started ringing. I flipped it over to see Jesse was calling.

"I am really pissed off at you right now. Bringing up Jack's past and talking about my assault with him is NOT okay! I will contact you when I am ready to talk to you again," I typed out through text message and sent it.

"I'm so sorry," she wrote back. It was the last thing I wanted to hear right now. I went to the cabinet in the kitchen and grabbed the bottle of wine I had opened on my first night here, the one I never really got to try since Jack interrupted me. Well, he wasn't going to interrupt me anymore. I popped the cork and drank as much as I could as fast as I could before drifting off to sleep.

I awoke to the sound of a door being shut. I could see lights shining through the windows. I ran to the window, seeing the taillights of a vehicle.

What the heck? I opened the front door to find an envelope with my name on it laying on the front step. I ripped it open. It was a letter from Jack.

Clara Kate,

I promise this is the last time you will ever hear from me. I just need you to know how awful I feel. I am such an idiot. You're right. I never even took your feelings into consideration. I think that's the part that hurts the most because you were all I was thinking about the entire time. Yeah, maybe the investigator side of me took over, but I swear I thought I was helping you. I've never liked a girl like you

who's filled with so much pain from her past that she can't see the possibilities of her future. You have no idea what it's like to be falling for someone that might not be able to give you what you hope for. I guess now we will never know.

Good luck on your next house sitting venture. I only wish the best for you.

Jack

Well, I had my final goodbye and now Jack has had his. Only, his hurt a lot more than mine. My goodbye was out of frustration and hurt. His goodbye in this letter is nothing but an apology and the best of luck to me. For some odd reason...right now...I hurt like hell.

I think I just pushed away the first guy to ever like me for the real me, plagued existence and all. *Did I overreact?* Regardless, I said what I did and I couldn't take it back. I laid back down on the couch and cried. I think this is what heartbreak feels like.

I cried myself to sleep in the wee hours of that morning. Tears of regret flowed down my face onto the couch cushion. Maybe if I had told Jack from the beginning that I never wanted anything to do with the man who raped me, I wouldn't feel the way I do right now.

****

The last few days of watching Mrs. Penney's house played out like any other movie where there's a girl who just went through a horrible breakup. I lounged around in my pajamas all day, eating every last cookie and brownie while watching reruns on the television. *We weren't even a couple, so why was I acting like we were?* He was just an acquaintance...a nobody.

When I packed up my stuff to leave, I found the scanner Jack had lent me in the very beginning of our friendship. He must have forgotten all about it. Maybe I could return it to him...or maybe I could turn it on just to hear his voice one last time. Yes, I will listen to it.

I heard my mom honking her horn in the driveway, so I locked the front door and left the key under the mat like I always had.

"Hey, Mom!"

"Hi, sweetheart. You are looking awfully tan. I hope you're remembering to wear your sunscreen."

"Of course! I wouldn't want skin cancer like your brother."

"Good! So what's new?"

"Not a whole lot. I'm excited about this new house. It's nice and small and I don't have a pool or hot tub to tend to."

"Like you need to relax anymore. You know, your brother can't believe you get paid to sit around all day. He actually started looking for house sitting jobs."

"Really? I don't just sit around. The other day I made brownies and cookies."

"Yeah. And then you sat around eating them."

"True," I said, both of us laughing.

"So how long is this next house?" she asked.

"Three months."

"I don't get it. Wouldn't it be cheaper to just get an alarm system installed?"

"They have animals like chickens, a dog and a couple of cats. Being gone for three months and all, it's just cheaper to hire a house sitter than to board all their animals."

"Oh. Well, won't the time frame interfere with you going off to college?"

I guess this is a good time to tell her the truth, so I took a deep breath in.

"I decided I'm not going to college."

"WHAT?" she yelled, startling me.

"Mom, calm down! College is not for everyone..."

"Look where I ended up! One dead end retail job after another!"

"It doesn't matter what you do in life. It just matters that you're happy doing it."

"Absolutely not! You don't know what you're talking about. You're too young! You're going to college and that's final!"

"Mom, it's too late."

"I saw the acceptance letters...lots of them!"

"That doesn't mean I accepted. I've known for a while I didn't want to go."

We pulled into the driveway of my next house sitting job and I jumped out, hoping she would let our conversation go.

"Don't think this conversation is over Clara Kate," she hollered, following me up the path to the front door of the house. I spotted the tractor pot with the pink plant in it right away, lifting it up and finding the spare key.

"Mom, there's nothing you can say or do that is going to make me change my mind."

"So what are you going to do then? This? This is not a job, Clara Kate. House sitting is baby stuff!"

"Really? Well this baby stuff has put a lot of adult money into my account. I'm going overseas."

"What the hell is that supposed to mean?"

"Paris...London...I'll go wherever people need me."

I glanced at my mother. She was speechless. Not only did my plans surprise her, I think they hurt her.

"What is so wrong with my idea?" I asked.

"You're throwing your entire future away. Is Jesse doing this too? Do her parents know?"

"Jesse is going to college and I'm happy for her, but I want to see the world."

"You are so naïve! You think you know everything, but mark my words, you will be sorry you didn't listen to your mother. That's what you do because mothers are always right."

"I'm sorry I've obviously disappointed you."

"You can pack up your belongings and get them out of my house then."

"What?" I asked, completely shocked by my mother's words.

"You heard me. I'm not going to be some storage unit while you're off traveling the world playing fa-la-la all day. You're an adult now, which means you go to work to pay your bills."

"Are you even hearing yourself right now? I am going to work, house sitting to pay for anything my heart desires."

"Get your stuff out so I can rent your room!" she snapped.

"Wow, that's nice, Mom. How am I supposed to get my stuff when you wouldn't even let me buy myself a vehicle to come and go as I please? I have to share one with Thomas, who doesn't even comprehend the meaning of sharing."

"You have one week!"

"What? That's ridiculous! Just throw it all away then."

"Don't get smart with me!"

"Seven days isn't enough to go through everything in my room from the last umpteen years when I have all these animals to take care of. Throw it all away, Mom, and rent out my room."

She turned and walked away, not even saying goodbye.

"Thanks for the ride," I hollered, but she didn't look back. *Wow. Jack, Jesse and now my mom.* I suddenly wish I were leaving right this second, far away from everyone so I could just be alone in peace and quiet. I can't believe what a bitch my mother just was. Kicking me out because I wasn't going to drive down the path she wanted me to pave! My oldest brother didn't go to college and she didn't kick him out. In fact, she let him and his pregnant girlfriend move in. *What a joke!*

Nobody was going to push me around and fit me into some mold they believed was suitable! Although I guess she could use the money renting out my room. My mother always worked so hard raising us three kids as a single parent. She still wouldn't tell me about my father. He was just a sperm donor to me. *Perhaps my brothers remembered him...*

I walked around the house, checking out the place. It was just a split-level ranch...nothing special. I found a small black and white dog in a black metal cage.

"Hey buddy," I said, leaning down and sticking my fingers through to let him sniff me. The owners were right, he was a friendly little guy. I let him lick my fingers for a couple minutes. "I'll be back for you," I said, wandering into the back yard. The chickens were walking all about, pecking at the ground. I tried to count them all, but gave up after reaching twenty-three.

I went back inside, wondering where the cats were. I began opening up doors until I found two of them in the downstairs bathroom. *Yikes*! *Let's change that litter box.* After I gave the cats fresh pooping grounds, I walked back upstairs, finding a note on the counter and reading it. When I flipped the note over, I saw a check for two thousand dollars. *Nice*! Not my biggest check, but it will definitely help me with my next chapter.

Jesse always dissed my house sitting career like my mother, saying I could make way more money working full-time even if I was making minimum wage, but I absolutely loved what I did. I couldn't say the same for Jesse or my mom.

My to do list was pretty simple; walk the dog, grab the mail, feed and water the animals, change the litter box and collect the eggs. Surely, I could do that for two grand! First, I took Rocky for a walk. According to the note, Rocky was a Boston Terrier and Bulldog mix. He was an easy dog to walk, stopping just a few times to complete his business. There were sidewalks which was even nicer. I had a feeling I was really going to like it here.

After a few days of the same old routine, I decided to bring out a lounge chair from the back yard to the front yard and start reading a new book. I tried to read in the backyard, but the chickens were far too distracting. Whenever they were ready to lay an egg, they made this loud clucking noise. Once one was done, another would start. One of them even landed on my leg and used it as a perch which scared the absolute daylights out of me. I mean, the note did say the chickens were very docile, but I was definitely a little afraid of them.

I heard a jingle jangle and looked up to see a man walking a dog. As they approached, my heart dropped. It was Jack. *What the hell was he doing here?* He never mentioned anything about owning a dog. I stuck my book up to my face as they passed. When they walked by, I knew I had to follow them. I ran into the house and put on my shoes, grabbing Rocky's leash and telling him it was time for a walk again. He was surely confused or not interested in another walk so soon, because I had to tug on his leash.

"C'mon, time for a walk. Let's go Rocky!"

I headed off in the direction I saw Jack go. When I got to the end of the road with no sign of him, I started wondering if my imagination was getting the better of me. I looked left and then right. Suddenly I saw a figure move. I could barely make him out, but I could see his bright red shorts. I had seen him wear those a couple of times.

I decided not to get too close, but I had to know what in the world he was doing here. *Did he live here? That would be too much of a coincidence. There's just no way! Or maybe it's a sign. A good sign or a bad one? Ugh, my mind is running away from me!*

I started down the road, then saw Jack turn into a driveway and he was gone. I got just close enough to see the house. It was light brown with dark blue shutters. The longer I stared, the more I wanted to walk up to the door and knock on it. No...I couldn't. Okay, I could, but I shouldn't. I said my piece and he said his. Before I left, I noticed the for sale sign out front. *Yup...this is his house, the one he bought with his ex-fiancé.*

So much for a fresh start away from Jack when he was living one street away. Life was full of surprises, that's for sure.

CHAPTER SEVEN

From that day forward, I walked Rocky every morning between six and seven knowing the chances of Jack being awake this early were slim. I turned the scanner on each night and each night when I heard his voice, I knew it was safe to take Rocky for a walk by Jack's house. I wouldn't go anywhere near there unless the scanner confirmed he was at work. I'd go by his house...stop and look in. I wondered what it was like to love someone so much you would buy a house with them. I hope someday I can say that.

What was I ever thinking getting involved with this guy? Look at this house! He was established.

"What do you think of this neighborhood?" I heard a woman ask, as I walked Rocky by Jack's house one evening. There was a husband, wife, two children and a lady dressed in a fancy suit. *Oh, a realtor. They must be looking to buy Jack's house.*

"It seems nice. I don't live in this neighborhood, though. I'm just house sitting."

"Oh, all right. Well, thanks!"

"No problem," I said, walking past. Today I didn't get to stop and stare. *What did it matter anyway?* It wasn't going to change anything. *Where would Jack go?* I have no idea where he'll move to. *Why can't I just get him out of my head?*

The next night I had forgotten to turn the scanner on until I heard sirens. I was turning into a nosy elderly woman, wondering where the police were going and what they were up to.

"Suicidal man barricaded himself inside house. Caller says he's been drinking. Neighbor confirmed there are weapons inside residence."

A few minutes went by as I nervously sat in the chair, twisting my hair with my right hand. Hardly anything exciting like this happened in our neck of the woods. Suddenly I heard a voice. "This is the St. Louis Police Department. Come out with your hands up." *What the hell was that?* I opened the back slider, taking the scanner with me. A minute later, I heard the same announcement over a speaker. *Oh no. This is close.*

"No response. We're going to need back up," a man's voice said over the scanner.

Shit! What if Jack is there? What if this man shoots a gun at him and kills him? I stood up, pacing back and forth, looking at the scanner for answers. I would never be the same if the words I said to Jack were the last I ever got to say to him.

After a few minutes of silence from the scanner, I leashed up Rocky. I would just walk by his house to see if he was home first. If he wasn't, maybe I would text him.

On my way out of the house, I noticed I forgot to put my sneakers on. *Focus, you idiot!* I ran back inside, looking all around the house for my shoes. I couldn't think under pressure, one of my least favorite traits about myself. All of a sudden, I heard a giant boom. *Shit*! I bolted full speed out the door, forgetting Rocky and my sneakers. *Screw it!*

Was that a gun? Did someone get shot? Did this man just commit suicide? I ran as fast as I could to Jack's house, probably looking like a suspicious lunatic to any neighbors watching me. I ran to the front door, my heart about to pound out of my chest and frantically knocked as hard as I could. After a moment of moving my hands all about, a nervous tic I developed as a child, Jack swung the door open. I leapt at him and wrapped my arms around his neck, squeezing as tight as I could. He fumbled backwards a few steps and then stopped. I could feel his warm hands on my back. I sobbed into the crook of his neck. *Thank God you're okay*. His armed moved from my back as he tried to lift me off him. I lifted my head from his tear-soaked shirt, grabbing his face and kissing him on his soft lips. After a moment, he set me back onto my feet. I was visibly shaking. *Woah, adrenaline*.

"I was so afraid. What was that loud noise? There's a guy that barricaded himself inside a house. Did you hear that announcement over the speaker?" I rambled.

A smirk played across Jack's face and then a woman turned the corner and stood in the doorway.

"Oh, hi..." I said, backing away from Jack. I looked from the woman to Jack and then back to the woman.

"Hi," she smiled, warmly. "I'm Jezebel."

Jezebel. Fiancé Jezebel. Wow!

"I'm the neighbor...down the street...all right...I'll talk to you another time." I turned to leave, my heart still racing and my legs wobbling like Jell-O.

"Wait," Jack said, but I was already out the door and onto the front steps. *Just go*! *He's safe*. I kept walking. I heard the door behind me as I made my way back down the path to the sidewalk.

"This is not what it looks like," Jack said, coming up on my side.

"She's...wow...nothing like me. Those legs and that makeup! Her hair is so long and perfect."

"Clara Kate. How did you find me?"

"I was listening to the scanner," I said, still trying to catch my breath. "Do you know what's going on?" I just wanted to get away from him. I felt so embarrassed. *So why was I still babbling?*

"Yes, they called me and placed me on alert in case I need to come in for back up. Is that what this is about?"

"No. Don't go into work...please...my heart can't take that." I kept walking.

"What are you saying?" he asked, but I didn't know what to say. "And why are you barefoot? What happened to your shoes?"

"It doesn't matter anymore," I replied, starting to cry again. I began to run. *Jack and Jezebel...the perfect pair. Then there was me. I had nothing. I had nobody.*

"Wait. Where are you going?"

I didn't stop. I just kept running. I ran back to the house, through the front door and tripped over Rocky, landing on the couch. I dug my face into the cushion and cried like a helpless newborn as Rocky whined and licked at my ear.

"What are you doing? Is this where you live?" I heard. I sat up to see Jack standing in the living room with his hands on his hips. I could feel my hair was a mess and my face was probably red from crying.

"No. I took the house sitting gig that was here in Missouri because it was down the street from your aunt's house. I knew I could still see you this way. This was before everything between us got so messed up!"

"Why do you just run away from everything?" he asked, frustrated.

"Because maybe that's all I know how to fucking do!" I grumbled.

"Well end it...right here, right now. You show up to my house out of the blue when I haven't heard from you in weeks! You're barefoot and crying and then just take off running down the street. C'mon, Clara Kate. What the hell is going on?"

"Just go back to Jezebel," I cried, instantly chastising myself for how immature I sounded.

"Forget Jezebel! She wants to get back together, but I, on the other hand, don't. She climbs into my best friend's bed and then what...the grass isn't greener on the other side so she wants me back?

Fuck that! She can be as gorgeous as she wants, but that level of disregard for the way I feel runs too deep."

"So, she really did leave you for your best friend?"

"Yes. I lost her and my best friend. Then I lost you."

I grabbed my knees and brought them to my chest, wrapping my arms around my legs.

"How did you know where I lived? Did my aunt tell you?"

"A few weeks ago, I saw you walking your dog. I was out front in this yard in a lounge chair reading a book. I swear I had no idea you lived in this neighborhood."

"That was you? What the heck, Clara Kate?"

"I wanted to talk to you. I followed you home that day, but I just couldn't. I wasn't ready."

"And now?"

"I thought you were at some house in St. Louis getting shot at. I freaked the fuck out when I heard that boom! Did you hear it too or am I just imagining this stuff?"

"That was just a flash bang smoke grenade they threw into the house," he said, as if it was no big deal.

"Well I didn't know," I said, feeling foolish.

"Come here," he urged. I shook my head no.

"Don't you have to get back to Jezebel?"

"Just come over here," he said. I shook my head again.

"Why?" he asked.

"Because I'm afraid I'm going to fall in love with you."

CHAPTER EIGHT

Jack's lips were on mine in an instant. His tongue danced along my sealed lips until I parted them, letting him know it was okay. His tongue teased mine, slowly moving in and out. It was such an unfamiliar feeling, but one that set my entire body on fire.

"If this is what being turned on feels like, I want to feel it all the time," I breathed, breaking away from our kiss. Jack let out a laugh. "Did I just say that out loud?"

"Yes. You mean, you've never been turned on before?"

"No. I guess not. Does that bother you?"

"Not at all."

"Okay...I want to be honest with you, Jack. I'm not really sure what pieces of me I can give you, but I know I want to try."

"Why are you letting me in?" he asked. "I mean, I could definitely see myself falling for you, but I'm just curious. Why me?"

"I don't know," I replied, not entirely understanding what it was that was drawing me to him either.

"There's something about your big strong hands and when they hold me. I feel like nobody can ever hurt me again."

"You make me feel like the luckiest guy in the world," he said with a giant grin.

"Do you really mean that?" I asked.

"Yes. Just the fact that you would give me a chance. I can only imagine the hurt that you have gone through, from feeling powerless to living in fear. I promise I will never make you feel that way," he said, grabbing my hand and holding it. The fact that Jack understood that this was a big deal for me made me want to cry all over again.

"I think I may have overreacted that day I blacked out. Seeing that man, it was all too real and I was so afraid that face was going to haunt my nightmares again. You have no idea how awful it was, trying so hard not to sleep because when you do, you wake up thrashing around, gasping for air...clothes drenched in sweat. I don't ever want to go back there."

"You can't begin to know..."

"No, I do know. I know that if you had this crystal ball and could see the future of that day, you never would've brought that picture."

"That was horrible. I'd rather be left at the altar any day...I really thought you were dead. You weren't seizing, but you weren't waking up either. I kept my two fingers on your neck, checking your pulse the entire time. I'm trained to stay calm, but that day...I'll admit I was freaking out," he said, running his fingers through his hair.

"Maybe you could tell me about him some time. That was definitely him in the picture, by the way. I've just had enough excitement for one day."

"All right. Well, you sit back and relax. I haven't gotten a phone call to go into work yet, so I'm probably not. I should go talk to Jezebel, though. She hadn't been there that long before you showed up and literally caught me off guard."

"Sorry I jumped on you," I chuckled. "I don't know what came over me."

"Don't apologize...it was sexy. Jump on me anytime." I smiled at Jack. I could feel my cheeks heat with embarrassment.

"So what are you going to say to Jezebel?"

"She'd like to know if she can move back in. She started talking about no longer wanting to sell the house."

"And?"

"I don't know. I mean, I guess she can move back in. It's half her house, even though we won't be together."

"Where will she sleep?"

"We haven't gotten that far. I'll go talk to her and I'll stop by later."

"Okay..." I said, not wanting him to leave.

"Don't say it like that. You're going to have to learn to trust me and to give me the benefit of the doubt."

"Okay. I'll see you later."

Jack leaned in and gave me a kiss. He pushed me back, pinning me against the couch as his tongue explored mine once more. *Oh, I could get used to this*. Then, he grabbed my face, stroking his thumb against my cheek and gave me a peck on the lips.

"Goodbye," he said, holding his face to mine and staring into my eyes.

"Bye."

Once Jack closed the door, I watched him walk down the walkway through the front window before I jumped off the couch and ran around the house, throwing fist pumps left and right. *Yes! Amen! Thank you! Is this love? Oh God, I hope this is love!*

I couldn't wait for Jack to return. While I waited, I decided to cook some dinner. *I'll make pizza!* I maneuvered around the kitchen, looking through all the cabinets until I found a Kitchen Aid mixer sitting out on the counter. *Perfect*! I can still remember my mother's dough recipe by heart. She would call during the afternoon every week asking if I wanted pizza that night for dinner. My answer was always yes because who didn't love pizza? She'd have me make the dough, so they were ready for her when she got home.

It was a no rise recipe which meant I could use it right away and get a nice thin crispy crust. The more it sat out for, the thicker and doughier the crust became.

I measured two cups of flour and then one teaspoon of salt. Then, I dissolved one teaspoon of yeast into a three-quarter cup of warm water. I stirred the yeast until it dissolved, combining all the ingredients and mixing it with the dough attachment for five minutes. *Viola*!

I found a can of sauce and some shredded cheese while the dough was mixing. I cut up some mushrooms and onions. The dough recipe made two pizzas, so with any luck, Jack will come walking back through that door when they are ready.

The house started smelling spectacular ten minutes into cooking. I cleaned up the kitchen and then turned the oven light on, peering in at my two master pieces. *Gosh, did I love pizza!* I could eat it every day.

When the timer beeped, signaling dinner was ready, Jack still hadn't showed, so I was forced to eat more than what I wanted to. I placed the leftovers in the fridge. I'd be eating pizza for the next few days! Feeling kind of sad and wondering what was taking Jack so long, I got into my pajamas, brushed my teeth and laid in bed. I could watch television in bed here which was a major plus since Mrs. Penney didn't have a television in her guest bedroom.

My eyes were just growing tired when I heard a knock at the door. I got up, noticing it was now dark outside. I found Jack on the front step holding a small duffel bag.

"Hey," I said.

"Hi."

"What's in the bag?"

"My stuff."

"For what?"

"I was hoping I could crash here tonight."

What? A sleepover with a guy? My mom would really be pissed at me now!

"Ahhh..."

Jack brushed past me and came inside.

"Apparently Jezebel isn't going to take no for an answer. She's sleeping in my bed. Well, our bed. I just can't even pretend like I love her...like that...anymore."

So, he still loves her...? I didn't know what to say.

"Well, I made some pizza earlier. I figured you would've been back for dinner, so I made way too much. Would you like some?"

"Yes, please! I just worked up an appetite going back and forth with Jezebel for the last few hours on what the plan was. I mean, she made it pretty clear she was leaving and we were selling the house. She even left her dog for me to take care of. Now, she's literally singing the complete opposite tune."

"And now?"

"I guess she's going to buy me out. She has to get a loan, though, so it might be awhile."

"What a mess..."

"I'll go back tomorrow. I just needed to get the hell away from her. It's like she wasn't hearing the word no when that's all she's told me since our wedding day. Shut down after shut down and now the tables are turned and she's not comprehending any of it."

"Would you be going back if you never met me?" I blurted out and then chastised myself for thinking I was that special to him.

"No. I'm not an idiot. People don't change. There's a certain timeframe for maturing and at twenty-four years old, she is who she is now."

"And what about me at eighteen years old? Do you think I can change?"

Jack let out a laugh.

"You tell me," he said, looking at me with a big smile.

"I hope so." *With all my heart.*

"Me too. Now, where's that pizza?"

I took the pizza out of the refrigerator and began heating up the oven. Jack grabbed the plate and started eating it cold. I shook my head at him, shutting the oven back off. *Cold pizza, ew!*

"This is the best crust ever. How did you get it so thin?"

"I don't let it rise. Why doesn't anybody know that trick?"

"Ooo...sorry Miss Deluxe Thin Crust."

I watched him devour slice after slice, wondering how he made something as simple as eating pizza look so desirable.

"I can't believe you just ate all that. I thought I had leftovers for the rest of the week!"

"You don't need it because I'll be taking you out."

"Really? Like on a date?"

"If that's what you want. Whatever you want, Clara Kate. I don't really want to get emotionally attached to you since you're leaving and although I'd beg you to stay, I just think your plan is perfect for you."

"Why do you say that?"

"Don't take this the wrong way, but your assault seems like it delayed you...not sexually. What I'm trying to say is that it seems like socially. I mean, anything we do it's like it's all brand new to you."

"I know what you mean. I think a lot of it is the fact that we were really poor growing up. My mom raised us all by herself."

"Where was your father?"

"I don't know. Something happened when I was five. I try to remember him, but I just can't. He was tall and skinny, but when I close my eyes, I can't see a face. I tried so many times to snoop through my mom's belongings, but I can't find anything. It's so weird."

"Well, why don't you ask her?"

"I have...maybe when I was ten or so. She just told me he was a traveling salesman who traveled far away from home and never came back. Nobody had seen or heard from him."

"And why are you just taking her word on it?"

"Because she was angry right before he left...furious, actually. She sent us all to our rooms and then I heard a bunch of shouting."

"I could try to find him for you. What's his name?"

"I don't even know. I guess that's a bit odd, isn't it? I don't even know my own father's name..."

"You've lived a most unusual life so far."

"You could definitely say that! Hopefully the rest of my life is a little less exciting."

"So, is there a blanket I could have for the couch?"

"I don't know. You can sleep in the bed with me as long as you don't touch me...like that. I'm not trying to sound like a jerk."

"I get it. Hands off."

"Sorry," I said.

"Don't be."

"Why are you so understanding? I don't get it."

"Because I really like you."

"So if you didn't, you'd be trying to get in my pants? Jesse said you only want me for sex."

"Jesse has no idea what I want. I don't even know what I want. If you wanted to have sex then I would, but since you don't then I won't. Just because Jesse meets guys that only want to use her for her body, doesn't mean she can place me in that category. Not all guys are pigs."

I could sense Jack's irritation. I went around the counter to where he was sitting and placed my hand on his shoulder. "I know. You are amazing. I couldn't ask for a better guy to spend my summer with."

"Bedtime?" he asked. I let out a laugh.

"Yes. Could you read me a bedtime story?" I giggled, sarcastically.

I laid in bed, watching Jack brush his teeth in the bathroom. Then he shut the door and I could hear him peeing. *This was SO weird!* This is what it would feel like if we lived together.

"Jack?"

"Yeah," he answered, opening the door and coming back into the bedroom. He crawled underneath the covers next to me. *Oh my gosh...I don't think my heart can take this*. Then, he took off his shirt and tossed it next to the bed. *Oh no...shirtless Jack in my bed. Cannot. Handle. This!*

"What were you going to ask me?"

"I can't remember now."

"What?" he laughed.

"Do you always sleep naked?"

"I'm not naked. I have my boxers on and some pajama pants. I usually just sleep in my boxers."

"Oh gosh, I don't think I could handle that!"

"I can put my shirt back on."

"No, it's okay. I don't even get why I feel the way I do. I mean, it's just a bare chest." *And those giant forearms!* "I saw both my brothers without their shirts on growing up all the time. You are just so...perfect. Your muscles...I've never been so turned on and now I have to sleep like this all night?"

"How do you think I feel every time I look at you?"

"Really?"

"Yeah! I got an instant hard on when you opened the door in your tight pink shorts."

"Don't talk like that!"

"Really? Sorry!"

"No...it's just turning me on even more. Maybe this was a bad idea! I'm going to bed," I said, abruptly turning over and closing my eyes, except I wasn't tired at all. I could feel my heart pounding. *My first sleepover...with a guy...a hot guy! IN MY BED!* I wish I wasn't such an awkward turtle. I craved the confidence I needed to have a normal adult relationship with this wonderful man laying inches away from me.

CHAPTER NINE

I opened my eyes just a smidge, seeing the sun peek through the sides of the window shades. Jack's arms were wrapped around me and I could feel something hard sticking into my back. I rolled over.

"Jack," I whispered. "There's something hard sticking into my back."

His eyes were closed, but a smirk played across his face. He rolled over.

"Sorry," he whispered back.

"Oh my gosh! Was that your...?"

"It's just excited to wake up next to such a beautiful girl," he said in his deep and sexy morning voice.

"Can I see it?"

"What?" he asked, turning back over and facing me. His eyes were wide open now.

"You have a boner right now?" I asked.

"Yes. It's called morning wood. Way to call me out!"

"I know what it's called. I took health class in high school. I just want to see what it looks like. I've never seen a penis before."

"That's like me asking you to see your vagina. Would you?"

"No. Fine...whatever. I was just curious, that's all."

Next thing I knew, Jack whipped the covers off, raised his pelvis to the ceiling and slid his pajama pants along with his boxers down. His erection sprang free.

"Holy shit!" I blurted out, covering my mouth.

"What?"

"That thing is huge!"

"Wow, way to build my confidence!"

"Seriously. How does a girl fit that thing inside of her? Does the whole thing go in or just part of it?"

Jack took a pillow and hit me over the head. We both laughed.

"Sorry. I'm probably being really annoying right now," I giggled.

"Are you going to ask me to cough for you too?"

"Huh?" I asked in confusion.

"When I go to the doctor, he squeezes my balls while I cough."

"So, you feel like I'm giving you an exam right now?"

"Pretty much. You haven't stopped staring at it. Would you like to touch it to?"

"Really?" I asked.

"Seriously?"

"Yeah. I kind of want to."

"Have at it," he said, laying back and staring up at the ceiling.

At first, I poked at the tip of his penis and he let out a noise.

"Did I just hurt you?"

"No," he chuckled. "Grab it like you mean it...don't poke at the guy."

"Sorry."

"Like this," he said, taking my hand and wrapping it around his penis. *Shaft, I think that is what they call this part.*

"Wow! It's so warm and squishy." I looked over at Jack who was still looking up at the ceiling smiling.

"How hard can I squeeze?"

"Like this."

"Oh my gosh, that's hard! I would've never squeezed you like that. I'd be too afraid to hurt you."

"No, it's pretty pliable. My balls on the other hand...you have to go easy on those."

"How come you don't have any pubic hair?"

"I shave. Don't you?"

"Yeah," I lied. *Note to self, I must shave.*

"How do you know about guys and pubic hair, anyway? I thought this is the first penis you've ever seen."

"Well, Jesse and I wanted to see what a black penis looked like when we were thirteen, so we used her mom's computer to find out when she left to go to the store one day. There was an entire slew of penis pictures we saw. I can't believe people had their body parts online for the whole world to see." I looked at Jack who was looking at me now. "What?" I asked him.

"You're adorable."

"I'm like a pre-teen stuck in an eighteen-year old's body."

"It's cute. I'll teach you anything you want to know."

"Really? You're not shy at all."

"I am. I feel really self-conscious right now, but knowing you don't have any other penis to compare mine to..."

"Are you circumcised?"

"Oh yeah. If I wasn't there would be this extra skin at the tip, right here," he said, pointing to the top of his penis.

"Oh, okay. Cool. So how does your boner go away now?"

"It doesn't."

"Oh my gosh, so then what? You have to walk around all day like that?"

"Gosh no. I'll just go to the bathroom and masturbate."

"Can I watch?"

"Hell no," he practically shrieked.

"Oh, sorry! I don't know the rules."

"Masturbate is when..."

"I know what masturbation means. I just wanted to see what it looks like. Is that strange?"

"No, it's actually really turning me on right now. I've just never masturbated in front of anyone before. It's kind of...weird."

"Oh, all right."

"You go like this, though," he said, taking my hand and firmly placing it on his penis. Together he slid our hands up and down his shaft with just a few strokes.

"Oh man...I better get going. I'm about to combust," he said, pulling his boxers and pajamas up and quickly heading towards the bathroom.

Hmmm...maybe I could use my hand to masturbate Jack. It seems easy enough. I got my phone, quickly typing out masturbating a penis. Underneath that was this word that caught my eye, fellatio. *What the hell was that?* I clicked on it. *Hmmm...oral sex involving the use of mouth, also known as a blow job. A blow job! How do you give one of those?* I quickly typed instructions on giving a successful blow job. I heard Jack start the shower and read through the instructions again. *I think I got this!*

I knocked on the bathroom door.

"Yeah?"

"Can I come in?" I asked, trying to sound confident.

"Sure."

"Hey," I said to the hot steam pouring over the blue shower curtain.

"You okay?"

"Yeah. Can I give you a blow job?" I asked, eager to see Jack's reaction.

"What?" Jack asked, whipping open the shower curtain and looking at me.

"I just want to say thank you for the sex 101 this morning."

"Clara Kate, you don't have to give me a blow job!"

"I want to..."

He shut off the shower, grabbing a towel and stepping out onto the bathmat. *Oh no, it didn't say how I would fit that entire thing in my mouth. Would I gag? I have an awful gag reflex!*

"How are you the only girl that's ever made me feel shy?" he asked.

I shrugged my shoulders and got down on my knees, grabbing Jack's penis and taking it into my mouth.

"Woah! Easy Clara Kate."

I ignored Jack's concern and kept going, shoving his penis to the back of my throat until I could feel my eyes start to water. I brought my head back and forth. I imagined I looked ridiculous right now, sucking on a penis popsicle, but maybe he wasn't watching. I looked up at Jack and his eyes met mine. *Oh, he's watching...*

"Don't stop," he said, bringing my head towards his penis again. *Mmm...I guess I'm doing it right*. I licked and sucked and stroked my hand up and down his shaft repeatedly. Just as my neck was beginning to hurt, I heard Jack moan. He grabbed the back of my head, his entire body going rigid. Warm liquid swirled around in my mouth and I swallowed it down.

"Holy fucking shit!" he gasped.

"Was that bad?"

"That was amazing! What the hell?"

"What?"

"I thought you had no idea what you were doing. That was hands down the best blow job I've ever had! You swallowed my cum?"

"Yeah. It tastes just like pizza crust."

Jack started laughing.

"Okay, some things you can keep to yourself," he said.

"Sorry."

"Don't apologize. You're an animal! You just completely caught me off guard. I was coming in here to masturbate all embarrassed you woke up to my boner in your back and then you knocked on the door and I thought something bad happened. Wow. That was just a great surprise!"

"I just wanted to say thanks for having patience with me."

"Well, you're welcome. This has by far been the most interesting birthday I have ever had."

"It's your birthday today?"

"Oops. I wasn't going to tell you because of the whole twenty-four years old age thing. Are you kicking me to the curb now?"

"No way! I want more penis in my mouth later on tonight."

"You can't say stuff like that."

"Why not?"

"It just gives me an instant boner."

"No, no more boners until tonight. We must go celebrate your birthday!"

I tip toed out of the bathroom, glancing over my shoulder and smiling mischievously before leaving. I will go cook Jack a birthday breakfast!

"Morning, Rocky," I said, opening up the cage and letting him out.

"Jack, I'm just going to take the dog for a walk and then I'll be right back to cook breakfast."

"Wait for me...I'll be two minutes."

"Okay." Just then Jack emerged from the bathroom wrapped in a towel and headed across the hall to the bedroom. *Ooo...that cute butt*. I poured myself a glass of orange juice and guzzled it down.

"Ready," Jack said, standing in the doorway.

"You look so hot and I look like a rag."

"You do not. Let's go!" Jack said, taking the leash from my hands.

"This is Rocky," I said to Jack. Jack bent down and pet Rocky who was all too excited for his morning walk.

"So, what do you want to do today?" I asked.

"Well, I have to work at three."

"That's lame."

"We can do something before...anything you want," he said.

"It's your birthday. Let's do whatever you want."

"You know what I want. How did you give such a good blow job anyway?"

I nervously looked around to see if any neighbors were out listening to our conversation.

"What?"

"I don't know. There's just hundreds of houses in this neighborhood, which means lots of people who could be listening."

"You're so paranoid. Nobody is out this early."

"Morning," a cyclist said, coming up from behind us and passing on our right.

"Morning," I said, giving Jack a dirty look.

"That guy was riding by so fast he has no clue what we were talking about. What were we talking about again?"

"Blow job. I googled it. I wanted to use my hand to masturbate for you, but then I saw the oral sex thing and it sounded pretty simple. I wasn't sure if I was supposed to swallow your semen, though. It was just an automatic reaction, I guess. What's in that stuff anyway?"

"I have no idea. Google it!"

"Okay."

"I'm kidding," he said.

"Already searching it. Semen ingredients." I looked at Jack who had stopped to let Rocky pee in the woods. He was smirking and shaking his head. "Ah ha! Semen is coined as the super food, made up of proteins as well as vitamins. Wow, there's a ton of vitamins listed here."

"Great! Now you can stop taking your multi-vitamin every morning and just suck me off."

"Very funny! Let's go home," I said, heading back down the street.

When we returned to the house, I started pulling out all the fixings for a birthday breakfast.

"Sit, I'll cook for you," he said.

"No way, it's your special day!"

"And I want to cook you breakfast. I never have anyone to cook for. Please?"

"Okay," I replied, sinking down onto the barstool.

"What are you going to make?"

"Well, those apples right there are telling me I should make some apple pancakes."

"Okay. That sounds amazing! Do you need me to look for a recipe?"

Jack pointed to his head. *Ah! He already knows one.*

"This was my grandfather's famous recipe. Every time I slept over his house growing up, he would make them for me."

"I can't wait to try them!"

I watched him move around the kitchen just like at Mrs. Penney's house, only I felt more confidence in his presence. I think somehow his penis show and tell ordeal this morning made us closer.

"I have to go to my aunt's before work. She wants to give me a present for my birthday, so I probably won't stay here long. I still have to go to my house, get my uniform and all that."

"Stay here," I blurted out.

"What do you mean?"

"Like...move in here. I don't really want you living with Jezebel. Do I sound like a crazy person? I kind of just want you all to myself until I leave."

"Okay."

"Yeah?"

"Yeah."

"So, when you get out of work, you will come here? Well, to your aunt's for the hot tub and then here?"

"I'll just come here after work."

"I don't want to ruin your routine at Mrs. Penney's."

"I kind of fibbed to you. I've only been to my aunt's once or twice after work. I really was going there to say goodbye to her the day we met, but I needed a reason to come back and see you again."

"Are you telling the truth right now? I mean, your aunt went along with it saying she told you that you could use the hot tub and pool anytime."

"She didn't lie. She did tell me that and I just stretched the truth. I go there to swim and relax in the hot tub, but hardly after work."

"Why did you want to see me again?"

"Well, you were sexy as hell for one thing. Standing there in your bikini all wide-eyed because you had a few sips of wine. It was really cute and innocent. I knew you were young and naive. There was something I just liked about that."

"Little did you know how undeveloped I was..."

"I know what you're saying, but please don't talk badly about yourself like that. You're immature sexually...yes, but you'll get there. You have confidence and that's half the battle."

"No, I don't. You couldn't be more wrong! I have zero confidence. Everything is so new to me and it's so annoying! I've had to listen to Jesse's sex stories for the last few years and the more I heard, the less confidence I had."

"Why didn't you just tell her to stop?"

"I don't know. I figured she'd catch on every time she told me about her next fling and I would sit there quiet, feeling uncomfortable, but she never did."

"Why uncomfortable? I mean, you just gave a blow job like an expert."

"That's oral sex. I think I can handle that. It's the actual penetration...I don't think I'll be able to do it. I really want kids someday, though. I don't know what to do."

"You're getting way ahead of yourself."

"I know. It just feels so good that you're here with me and my mind is running away with ideas."

"I could think of one."

"What?" I asked, finding two plates and setting them at the counter.

"How about I return the favor?"

"To me? My vagina?"

"Yeah. It's called eating you out or carpet munching."

"Eww! Carpet munching? That is just too gross sounding."

"It will feel really good. Have you ever orgasmed?"

"No and I don't think I'm ready yet...for the carpet thing, but I'll let you know when I am."

"Okay," he said, sliding some pancakes onto our plates and chuckling.

I couldn't stop looking at Jack as I ate my pancakes. In this moment right now, life was imperfectly perfect. I just got kicked out and I still wasn't talking to my best friend, but I was sitting next to Jack and that made everything in my life seem okay.

"So, how do you know my aunt? I mean, I get that she was your teacher, but how did you get to watching her house?"

"Well, long story short, she's a psychology teacher as you probably already know and I was in her class my sophomore year of high school. This was when I gained all that weight and I was going to school like a zombie. I was a good student and every time she called on me I knew the answer, so she liked me. Well, when it came time to learning about trauma, she touched on sexual assault. Little did I know the entire week was about molestation, rape, human trafficking; you name it, she discussed it. Everyday I would get to her class, raise my hand and go to the nurse because I didn't feel well. I wasn't lying either, I felt nauseous and I was so afraid of another panic attack, but in front of my classmates this time. I usually had them at home at night."

"So then what?"

"On the last day that week, Friday, she came down to the nurse's office when class was over. I'll never forget it. She shut the door without a word and sat down on the bed, taking my hand in hers. She said, 'You don't have to tell me what happened, but I really hope you do.'"

"What did you do?"

"I balled my eyes out while she held me. I don't know how she knew. I thought maybe it was some maternal instinct."

"She doesn't have any children."

"I know. I learned that after."

"So you told her that day?"

"Yes. I let it all out and it felt so good. I had been holding it in the entire time. She was really comforting...almost like she could feel my pain. It was weird. Anyway, I started seeing her after school, like my very own psychologist. I told my mom I was staying late for extra help. Mrs. Penney told me I was sheltering myself too much and I needed an outlet. She told me she was going away like she does every summer and wanted to know if I would like to stay at her house, just to get away from the norm. I tried it and the rest is history."

"Wow, that's crazy!"

"Yeah. Just because your aunt knows what I've been through, though, doesn't mean I want you to go talk about me to her. Okay?"

"Okay."

"That reminds me. I'm sorry I told Jesse about your past. You were right, I shouldn't have said anything," I said.

"She really caught me off guard that day, walking outside and telling me she's sorry for my son's death. I just don't go telling everyone 'Hi, my name is Jack and my son died.'"

"I know. I told her I thought we were a good match because we carried the same amount of pain. It was stupid and I apologize."

"All is forgiven. I'm just glad you forgave me, that's all."

"About that. How did you find him...the man...?"

"Well, after Jesse was all sorry about your boy and your fiancé, I asked her where you guys were camping when you were sexually assaulted. I know you said you didn't tell Jesse much, so I didn't even know if she knew you were raped."

"She knows..."

"Well I just asked her what campground you stayed at."

"And?"

"And then I looked it up. That's how I got the town and then I started looking through rape cases in that area that occurred four years ago. I actually found a lot of men charged with rape, but he was the only one who stood out to me with the jet-black mustache you described and clean shaven everywhere else."

"Wow."

"Did you tell me he was a serial rapist?" I asked.

"That just means he raped more than one and yes, he raped a total of fourteen girls. Not women...girls."

I placed my hand over my mouth, taken aback by Jack's words. Maybe if I had come forward, he could've been stopped.

"How?"

"Campgrounds. The same way he assaulted you. The odd thing was that each case was after that summer...almost like you were his first victim. It was the summer when you were fourteen, right?"

"Yes."

"Yeah. I'm pretty sure everything documented was after your incident. He was finally caught when this little girl was in the shower and her mother was using the bathroom in the same facility. I found the names and googled the story. The mother was actually constipated. I know...sounds weird, right? But it said whenever she went on vacation she would get constipated from eating differently. Anyway, she was on the toilet for at least ten minutes trying to pass a bowel moment, or so the story read. There were two exits to the bathroom and the man mistakenly thought she had entered with her daughter through the front and exited without her daughter through the back."

"So do you think he had been watching me that night?"

"Oh yeah, without a doubt."

"That is so creepy! I had no idea what was about to happen going in there, but he did. Probably hiding behind a tree." I shuddered at the thought.

"Well he's behind bars now and he was not a police officer. I just have to make that clear."

"How did he get that uniform?"

"Are you kidding me? You can buy anything you want off the internet!"

"It looked so real, though. I've hated cops for years. What's the background story on the guy?"

"I didn't get that far, but I can look into it for you."

"I think I'd like to if you can give me his name."

"Sure."

Jack and I spent the rest of the day relaxing in each other's company. I showed him the chickens and how to collect the eggs. He hugged and kissed me every chance he could get. I wondered if he was falling for me as fast as I was falling for him. He was like a dream. I had never felt so comfortable with anybody. I was always on high alert, even at the mall with Jesse, but with Jack...I completely let my guard down. I was carefree. I felt like an entirely different person.

"Can I make you an egg sandwich for lunch?" I asked.

"Sure. Then I really have to go."

"Boo," I said, making a sad face and pouting my lips.

"Yeah...okay, Clara Kate. How do you think I am going to feel when you move thousands of miles away and I never see you again?"

"Let's just live in this moment."

"That's the plan," he said, staring off in deep thought. I knew what he was thinking about, two more months, sixty days until we would part ways, but I wasn't going to give up my dream for him. I didn't want to stay in Missouri. I never felt like I belonged here.

We dug into our breakfast sandwiches. I was waiting for him to ask me why I was making eggs for lunch, but he never did. Jack never questioned anything I did unless we were in a deep conversation, which was nice.

"Eggs are such a weird concept," he said.

"What about them?"

"Well, a chicken just poops an egg out, but potentially, this egg could hatch and become a chicken, so basically we're eating a fetus."

"Really? This was really good too," I said, placing my egg sandwich down and sliding my plate away from me.

"C'mon, you're not going to not eat just because of that?"

"I don't want to eat a baby! That's disgusting."

"I'm finishing all of mine. Can I have yours too?"

"There's something very wrong with you!" I said, laughing.

"Oh stop! It's just a part of life. Besides, they have no rooster to fertilize the eggs so technically none of these eggs would hatch if a hen sat on them."

"I don't know, but I'm weirded out now. I'll eat something else after you go."

"You better get over it because I'm going to need some more brownies and cookies soon."

Jack grabbed me, catching me off guard. He picked me up over his head and twirled me around. I threw my head back and let a laugh escape that I had never heard before.

"Ugh, I don't want to leave you right now," he breathed.

"Then don't. Cancel with your aunt and then call in sick."

"I can't. Goodbye," he said, kissing me on the nose and leaving. *Ugh, Jack was too responsible*! I was a bad influence.

I got right down to business making Jack a birthday cake. *What kind did he like? Chocolate or Vanilla? I'll make both!* When it came time to frost them, I did half chocolate frosting and half vanilla on both. I literally couldn't go wrong here! I wrote the generic *"Happy Birthday!"* on one cake and *"To A Man Worth Walking On Glass For!"* on the other cake. If he didn't like cake, then at least he'd get a good laugh from my ripe sense of humor.

The day dragged on after that. I couldn't wait for Jack to return. I took Rocky for his evening walk and then it dawned on me; I would try shaving my pubic hair. Here I was, standing in the shower, deathly afraid to take a sharp razor to such a sensitive part of my body. *I mean, what's the worst thing I could do? Cut myself so deep I couldn't pee...no...not possible.*

I lathered up my public hair like I did my legs every time I shaved them. *Ouch...this doesn't feel too good.* I looked around for any signs of blood, but didn't see any so I kept going. By the time I was finished, I had an entirely new look. *Why did guys like this? It looked like I had a little girl's vagina...hairless. Did this mean I was ready for the carpet thing? Maybe*.

By the time I shaved my legs and continued on to my armpits, my fingertips were like raisins from being in the water for so long. I got out of the shower, dried myself off and laid in bed wrapped in my towel. Maybe I'd stay like this and surprise Jack when he gets home. Or maybe I'll take my towel off and he can find me sleeping...naked.

I let my towel fall to the floor and got back underneath the covers, turning on the television and flipping through the channels until I landed on my murder mystery show. I moved my legs back and forth across the mattress. I felt so free being naked underneath the covers.

I must've drifted off because I awoke to find Jack on top of me kissing my cheek.

"You left the door unlocked," he whispered in my ear.

"For you," I said, moving my head until my eyes locked with his.

"Don't do that again. I want to keep you safe."

I wriggled out from underneath his weight and rolled onto my side.

"I need to give you your cakes and sing happy birthday. I didn't know what kind you would like, which is why I made you two."

"I just found them on the counter! Delicious, Clara Kate, but just coming here after work and being with you is enough."

"I don't know about that..."

"What do you mean?"

"You haven't gotten underneath the covers yet," I said, giggling.

"I haven't had the chance," he said, scooching off the bed and undressing. *Oh, I could watch this all day.* After he stripped down to his boxers, he grabbed his pajama pants.

"You probably won't be needing those."

"Okay," he said, tossing them on the floor. I followed him with my eyes over to the bathroom to watch him brush his teeth just like the night before. *Was I being too bold?* This was the part where I acted like I had confidence, but inside I was a nervous wreck. I was like a little kid on Christmas, waiting for the anticipation.

Jack slid underneath the covers and made his way over to me, wrapping his arm over my chest.

"What the..."

I was full on laughing now.

"Are you completely naked right now?"

"Happy birthday to you..." I sang.

"You are the best..." he said, kissing my forehead. "The greatest..." he said, kissing my neck. "The sexiest," he said, kissing in between my breasts. "And the funniest woman I have ever met," he said, kissing me on the lips.

"I shaved."

"Can I feel?"

"I guess. I'm really shy..."

"Wow, nicely done, Clara Kate," he said, smiling. I wanted to put a pillow over my face. *Oh...oh God help me...*the sensation from his fingers dancing over my pubic bone sent electrifying shocks throughout my entire body.

"Oh, I get it. Are you my cake tonight?"

"Bingo!"

"Can I give you your first orgasm?"

"What does it feel like?"

"Pure ecstasy."

"What if I don't get one?"

"Then I didn't do a very good job."

I looked around the room, anywhere but at Jack.

"You're not broken. You'll orgasm, trust me. Just lay back, close your eyes and enjoy."

"But it's your birthday," I said, lifting my head up off the pillow to see Jack pulling back the covers.

"Can we shut the light off...please?" I asked.

Jack stood up from the bed and walked towards the wall, shutting off the light. I could feel him return to the bed. I laid back down, my heart about to beat out of my chest.

"Ready?" he asked.

"Just do it," I replied.

I heard him snicker and then felt his tongue...THERE...ON MY LADY BUSINESS. *Oh. Lord. Have. Mercy. This feels good...SO good*! I clenched my hands into fists and grabbed at the bed sheet. Something was happening...a feeling down there I had never experienced before. My legs were growing weaker by the second and then...*oh...oh my...wow...oh yeah, okay. Holy shit!* My body shuddered uncontrollably as the sensation continued.

Jack lifted himself off me and made his way up towards my head.

"How was that?" he asked, casually.

"That was insane...absolutely mindboggling...best feeling I have ever had!"

"Good."

"Would you like another awesome blow job?" I panted, trying to steady my breathing.

"Actually...I think I'd like to end my birthday holding you in my arms until you fall asleep, if that's okay."

"Okay," I said, confused. Jesse was all wrong about Jack. She couldn't have been more wrong. *When I offer a second blow job, he turns it down to snuggle?* As I lay there, I felt a wave of pain crash through my heart. Out of everyone I'll leave behind, I think I'm going to miss Jack the most.

CHAPTER TEN

From that day forward, Jack and I had developed a routine together. We would wake up, take Rocky for a walk, I'd tend to the cats and chickens while Jack cooked us breakfast. We'd take showers... separately, since the last place I would want any form of intimacy would be a shower stall. Then, we would head out and run errands or go do something fun like mini golf.

Jack taught me the erotic meaning behind the number sixty-nine, which was my new favorite number. He never brought up a relationship status, which was nice, but I sure did feel like he was my boyfriend.

I knew in the back of my mind that I had to face Jesse. I had been blowing her off for far too long. I think deep down I just wanted to get to know Jack better without Jesse meddling in our relationship. She had met him for all of sixty seconds before she managed to interfere.

I sent her a text. "Hey! Would you like to go out to lunch this week? I really miss you." It was the truth. As angry as I was with Jesse, I still thought of her daily, multiple times a day. She was a part of me.

"Sure. I miss you too. Tomorrow?"

A smiled played across my face. I texted Jesse the address and she replied back saying she would be there around noon.

I waited to tell Jack until the following day, just before Jesse arrived and then left quickly after I saw Jesse's car pull into the driveway. I didn't want to leave any time for Jack and Jesse to converse. *Was I afraid she would try to go after him? Was I afraid he would see something in her that I was sorely lacking?* I didn't know.

"Hey."

"Hey. Whose car?" Jesse asked.

"Jack's. Long story, but he's kind of staying here with me right now."

Jesse tried to hide her shock, but I knew her all too well.

"So, you two..."

"Made up, yeah."

Jesse backed down the driveway and we left.

"Where did you want to eat?" she asked, pretending not to be curious about Jack.

"I'm craving something light like a salad, so anywhere will work for me," I replied.

"Let's do that all American on the corner downtown."

"Okay. So what's new?" I asked, half wanting to know and the other half reserved.

"Just getting ready for college. I made a check list and I'm trying to complete a little every day. It's super overwhelming."

"Are you excited, though?"

"Oh yeah! This past month I've gotten a taste of what it's going to be like without you and I'm really bumming. I'm going to miss you."

"I know. I've really missed you. I just needed a time out in life."

"What have you been up to?"

"I've been hanging out with Jack a lot. I really like him."

"Like friends or boyfriend and girlfriend?"

"Friends I guess."

"What do you mean 'I guess.' Have you guys been...you know...intimate?"

"Not really."

"Don't think I don't know when you're purposely being vague in order to hide something. I'm onto you."

"Well, we've fooled around...everything except for...that. I don't know if I'm ready. How did you know you were ready?

"I wanted to know what it felt like."

"Well I know that..."

"No...not at all. Rape and sex are two very different things, Clara Kate. Don't confuse the two. I'm sure if Jack is the one then he'll be slow and sweet."

I tapped my right foot on the passenger side floor of Jesse's car, eagerly wanting to change the subject.

"So, how's dating life for you?" *Ugh, why did I just ask her that?*

"I've met a few new guys. Nothing special like yours..."

"Why do you think Jack is special?"

"For starters, he's still with you. I mean, the whole sexual assault thing would be enough to scare most guys off. So obviously he's patient and understanding. Plus, he's older and has a real job...the whole maturity thing."

"I'm mature," I blurted out, completely forgetting that we weren't even talking about me here.

"I don't mean it like that. I would just think that he's ready to settle down and start a family. You're fresh out of high school and ready to experience the world. Besides, that day I met him and we were talking, you came out onto the back patio and his face lit up like a firework on the fourth of July. I'll have to admit I felt a little jealous. I hope someday a guy looks at me that way. He's definitely special!"

"You'll find someone..."

"I hope you're right," Jess said, pulling into the restaurant parking lot. We got out and went inside. I ordered a Caesar salad and Jesse ordered a hamburger. Jesse was as small as I was, but boy could she eat! She didn't exercise either so I'm not sure how she stayed so thin. *Maybe all the sex...*

"Can we never go this long without talking again?" she whined, when we were through with our lunch.

"Yes!" I replied.

"Promise?"

"I promise! Besides, I think I violated like ten different girl codes and I'm lucky you're even talking to me."

"You're my better half, Clara Kate. So, when is your last day here?"

"I'm not sure. I haven't actually booked my next house sitting job. I've been looking, but nothing sounds appealing just yet. Do I want a short stay in case I don't like it there or long in order to figure out my next move?"

"Aren't you going to miss Jack?"

"Yeah. I think that's partly why I haven't found my next house. Once I do, it's like the clock will start." *Tick tock, tick tock*. "I don't think I'm ready just yet."

"Well you better figure it out and fast."

"I know because my mom kicked me out."

"WHAT?"

"Sorry, I forgot that part. I told her my plans after the summer and let's just say she wasn't a fan."

"Wow. I never saw that coming. You know you can always stay in my room. My parents would be totally fine with it."

****

I noticed Jack's car was gone when I returned home. I hugged Jesse goodbye, unlocking the front door and going inside. I called Jack.

"Hey, baby," he said, picking up on the first ring.

"Hey. I just got back home. Where'd you go?"

"My house."

Huh?

"Cool. What are you doing?"

"Just packing up some of my things. Figured I better take advantage of the opportunity. Once Jezebel gets approved, I'll be out."

Was Jezebel there? I wanted to ask, but I didn't want Jack to know how jealous I was. Suddenly I heard a female's voice in the background. *Errr*!

"So what are you doing with all your stuff?" I asked.

"I'll leave it here for now and once my name is off the loan, I'll put it in storage."

"All right, well...I guess I'll let you get back to it."

"Want me to come back?"

"No," I lied and sat down on the couch to sulk.

"Okay. I'll see you later."

"Bye," I said, hanging up the phone before I could let Jack respond. *Why did I get so crazy every time he went near his own house? Ah!* Jealousy was a very real thing. It made me feel like a crazy person. Not only did I not have any control over the situation since we weren't in a relationship, but I had to put my trust in him that he would no longer do to Jezebel what he did to me...almost every night.

Just the thought of him giving her oral sex was putting my anxiety at an all time high. *Did she give him a good blow job? He said I was the best*. I tried to read the book I had started last month, but my mind was so preoccupied I kept reading the same page.

I decided to take a warm relaxing bath. I closed my eyes and laid there, feeling the weight of the world on my shoulders. As the water turned cold, I heard my name being called just beyond the door.

"In here...bathroom."

"Now that's a sight to see," Jack said, glancing down at my naked body in the bathtub.

"Hi," I said, smiling shyly. "All done packing?"

"Hardly."

Damn it!

"Why's the front door unlocked? I really want you to start locking it. Did you even hear me come in?"

"No."

"See? Start right now and lock the damn door! Do you know how many home intrusions I've gotten called to just this year?"

I laid there batting my eyelashes at him.

"Cute," he said. "I was just saying goodbye before I go to work." Jack sat on the edge of the tub. I grabbed his hand and brought it to me.

"Stay," I said, holding his hand over my vagina, "and we can play." Jack put two fingers inside me, creating circular motions that sent shivers down my spine.

"Tempting, but I can't. I have to go...right now...or I'll be late," he said, pulling out of me.

"Wow! That was really mean."

"Just getting you ready for tonight. You better be waiting for me."

"Ha!" I said, laughing. "In your dreams...I'll be sleeping when you get home. Too-ta-loo!"

Jack kissed me on my lips and then left the bathroom. I drained the tub, grabbed a towel and ventured to see if he had locked the door. Oh yeah, he locked it. I suddenly wondered how many rape calls he had taken. Then I questioned if I had called 9-1-1 that night, if the man who raped me would have been caught. *Would it have made a difference? Ugh, I have to stop thinking about this! Would these thoughts forever be engraved in my mind?*

The night went like every other night where I was waiting for Jack to return home. I lounged around, ate some dinner, took Rocky for a walk and laid in bed watching television until I fell asleep.

I woke up to the weight of Jack's body lying on top of me.

"You look so precious when you sleep," I heard him whisper, kissing me on my cheek.

"How was work?"

"Good. Uneventful..."

"Uneventful is definitely good," I said, slipping out from underneath the covers and going to the bathroom.

"Hey, where are you going? I want to snuggle you."

I giggled while closing the door. I checked myself in the mirror, yikes! My hair was a little disheveled, but the lights would be off for what I had in mind. It was time. I wanted to take things to the next level. My mother always told me to hold off on any sexual intercourse until I found someone special. Jesse's words played in the back of my mind... "Just try," and "Jack is special." I brushed my teeth and went back to bed where I found Jack undressed and under the covers waiting for me.

"So, I was thinking..."

"Oh here we go," he said, teasingly.

"Oh hush! I think I'm ready to try having sex."

"Yeah?"

"Yeah. I mean...if you want."

"Well, if this is a yes or no question, then it's definitely yes," he said, laughing.

"I'm nervous, though and don't know what to do."

"Just lay back."

"I hate that...when I don't know what's going to happen and you do..."

"I can lay back and you can take control."

"No...no. I don't know what I'm doing."

"You didn't google...you know, different sex positions?"

"Should I?"

"Clara Kate! I'm kidding...lay back and enjoy."

"Will you just go slow?" I asked, laying onto my back. Jack moved over and looked down at me.

"I get it," he said, placing his hand over mine. *Ugh, Jack was the sweetest guy I could ever imagine. How the hell was I ever going to find someone that was half as wonderful as this man?*

"What are you doing?" I asked when he got off the bed.

"Getting a condom from my wallet. No, it's not whatever you are thinking. I put it in there before I even met you."

Life before Clara Kate.

"We never talked about STD's..." I said.

"And you want to do that right now, at this very moment?"

"Maybe?"

"I've only slept with two people; Jamison's mother and Jezebel. I would tell you if I had an STD."

"Have you even been tested?"

"Of course."

"Okay...did I ruin the moment? I'm sorry."

"No, talking about STD's really makes me want to have sex with you," he joked, sarcastically. He climbed on top of me completely naked. "I'm kidding...nothing would stop me from wanting this." He bent down and kissed me, pushing his tongue through my lips and making his way inside my mouth.

Just kissing Jack had me completely flustered, but then his fingers wandered down over to my right breast and then the left. His mouth followed, taking my nipple with his tongue. *Oh...my...gosh! Who knew that felt so good? Oh wow.* When he was finished with that nipple, he made his way over to the other while slipping his fingers inside me.

"Jack..."

"You okay, baby?"

"I'm about to explode. Can we skip this part? Seriously, that nipple thing is unbelievable."

"Okay," he chuckled. He made his way back up to my head, kissing me again. Then, he parted my legs wide and bent down, slowly entering my vagina.

Okay...it's in. I'm okay. Phew! I can do this!

Jack started out nice and slow which felt beyond amazing and then with each thrust, he started to increase his pace. Somewhere the pleasure started turning to pain. My anxiety presented itself and I began to panic.

"Are you okay?" Jacked asked.

"No," I sobbed. Jack quickly pulled out of me and rolled over.

"What happened?"

"I don't even know," I cried. "I thought I was okay and then it hurt and my chest grew tight. I'm so afraid I'll have a flashback."

"Why do you do this to yourself?" he asked, getting off the bed and flicking on the light. I sat there feeling defeated as I watched him dispose of the condom and put his boxers back on. "This isn't a fucking competition...let's see how far you can go. Obviously you aren't ready," he grumbled.

"I'm sorry..."

"It just feels like you're on this fucking mission all the time. You just use me to see how far you can take things because you're never going to see me ever again. Everything we do...it's all for the next guy that comes along..."

"That's a really cruel thing to say," I said, sitting up and wrapping the sheet over my bare chest.

"It's the truth, isn't it? I was fine doing what we were doing. I don't need to have sex...you know this. I just don't get it with you."

"Just go..."

"What?" he asked, surprised.

"Go be with someone who isn't so fucked up."

"Stop!"

"Just get out...please. I can't give you what you need!"

"I'm standing here right in front of you and you're not even listening to me!"

I turned my head away from him, looking at the wall.

"Fine...have it your way..." he said, grabbing his clothes and leaving the bedroom. After a moment, I heard the front door slam shut.

Shit! Why did I just do that? Jack was the greatest guy I had ever met. I laid down, closing my eyes and running through the words he had just said. *A mission? Using him to see if I was able to have intercourse? It wasn't true!* I couldn't even picture another guy coming along that would make me feel half as special as how Jack makes me feel.

I rolled onto my side, continuing to stare at the wall and wondering how long Jack felt like I had been using him. His words made me feel sad and at the same time, they made me feel bad that he felt that way. That was never my intention.

I wasn't sure how long I had been laying there frozen by my thoughts when I saw the light from the hallway peer into the bedroom. Before I could turn to see who it was, Jack was laying next to me on top of the covers. He wrapped one of his arms around my waist.

"I'm sorry," he whispered in my ear. Fresh tears sprung to my eyes. "Before I met you, I thought I knew what love was. I was such a fool. This is love...you and me. I've seen you vulnerable so many times and you are still perfect in my eyes."

I turned over and laid on my back, looking into Jack's eyes.

"Telling me to go be with someone else rips my fucking heart out. There's nowhere else I'd rather be, Clara Kate. I'll take you any way I can have you."

I reached my arms up and grabbed Jack, pulling him down on top of me.

"I'm sorry I said those things," I said. Jack hugged me back. "Do you really feel like I use you?"

"No...I just said that because I was pissed off. You have this idea in your head that I need sex. How many times do I have to tell you that I don't? I don't care what Jesse said or what anyone fucking says."

"Okay," I said, grabbing Jack's face and kissing him. "I just want you to be happy."

"I am happy. You have no idea how happy I am when I am with you."

"I get so afraid that I'm holding you back. You could be out meeting all these girls..."

"I'm just not an 'all these girls' kind of guy. Besides, when you leave, I can meet plenty of new chicks."

"Very funny," I said, punching his arm.

"I love you," he said.

"How do you know? I obviously have no idea what that is. I mean, I love my mom, but my heart doesn't flutter when I see her the way it does every time I look at you."

"Really? What else happens when you see me?"

"I think about you even when you're right in front of me. It's like from sunrise to sunset, all these thoughts of you are zooming around in my head," I confessed. "What do you think about?"

"How much I'm going to miss you. I can have my cake, but I can't eat it too and that's a hard reality for me most days." I couldn't help but cry. Jack was such a catch twenty-two for me. I could have the perfect guy, but just for one summer.

"How do you know it's love? I mean, you asked Jezebel to marry you. You bought a house with her! Do you even know what it is?"

"It's when you would do anything for someone."

"Then come with me."

"Clara Kate...these are my home roots. This is where I feel most comfortable because it's all I know."

"It's weird that Jezebel left you, saying it was because she wanted to travel more and that wasn't your dream. Now she's trying to buy your half of the house. I mean, so much for traveling when she is settling down. I think if you could've just removed your best friend from the picture, you and Jezebel might have been okay."

"I don't know. I think people have these thoughts in their head and then when they aren't what they pictured them to be, they go back to the only thing they know."

I laid there in Jack's arms, my favorite place to be.

"If traveling the world isn't what you pictured it to be, then I hope you come back to me," he said.

"Deal."

"Really?"

"Yeah. I have no idea...I could last a week and hate it. Or a few months. What about a year?"

"No matter what, I want you to come back to me."

"And if you're married with children?"

"I don't see that happening within a year. Go to bed," Jack said, yawning. He got off the bed and took his clothes off.

"Just seeing your body turns me on every time. Do you work out?" I asked.

"When I can."

A devilish look played across my face right before I threw the covers over my head and inched my way down to Jack's penis. I pulled down his boxers, happy to see he had already managed to get an erection. I didn't take his penis into my mouth right away. I licked and sucked as I made my way up and down his long shaft. I heard Jack moan; a reward that let me know I was doing a good job.

After a minute, I took Jack's penis into my mouth and began my torturous tongue lapping that would have his teeth clenched and panting "oh fuck" within minutes. I worked through the pain in my neck, happy to pleasure such a patient man. Within minutes I could feel Jack pulsating beneath me and then the warm rush of liquid pouring into my mouth.

Jack whipped the covers off my head.

"You are a goddess!"

"Sleep like a baby," I beamed, rolling over and shutting my eyes.

"Now I will," he laughed, grabbing me and pulling me tight against his body. "I love you. I love you. I love you," he said, kissing my head.

"I love you too."

CHAPTER ELEVEN

The next morning, I woke up to Rocky whining. I checked the time...*shit*! It was almost nine o'clock. I nudged Jack, letting him know I'd be back.

"I'm getting up," he groaned, rolling over and sitting up.

"We didn't get to bed till very late...sleep."

"No. I want to spend every minute I can with you."

"You're breaking my heart when you say things like that."

"Then don't go," he said, putting on a white cotton t-shirt and basketball shorts. "Just be with me."

"Don't do that. You have to let me go. I have no future here."

He didn't say a word. I watched him walk out of the bedroom, leaving me with my thoughts. *I better hurry up and find my next house, so my plans are set in stone.*

"You ready?" Jack called.

"Coming!"

Rocky was a great dog. I would surely miss him when I left. I'd miss all the animals, actually. They were such easy animals to care for.

"Jack," I said, halfway through our walk, "would you like to go to my mother's house with me next week? She's invited me for dinner."

"Sure. I'll let you take me home," he said. I smiled at him. I tried to take Rocky's leash. After all, I was the one getting paid to walk him. Jack refused to let me walk Rocky, saying he didn't mind.

"I know we're not girlfriend boyfriend, so if it's too weird..."

"Really? I tell people I have a girlfriend all the time."

"You do?"

"Yeah. I just had a woman ask if I was available the other day."

I stood there silent, not sure what to say. I wondered what he will tell them once I leave.

"So we're having a scheduled breakup in a month?" I laughed, but it was anything but funny. In fact, I had to fight the tears from making their way to the surface.

"Yeah, I guess," he said, with a laugh just as fake as mine.

I called my mother right when Jack left for work, asking her if I could bring my boyfriend. She was speechless. I thought for a moment the line had gotten disconnected, but then she told me she'd be delighted to meet him. When I hung up, I started second guessing myself. *Was this a good idea?*

By the time my mother's Farewell Clara Kate dinner rolled around, I had overanalyzed every possible thing that could go wrong. My loser brother might be there and would treat me like dirt in front of Jack who would definitely not stand for that. My mother's food would be inedible.

****

"Are you nervous?" Jack asked on the ride over to my Mom's house.

"Very."

"There's nothing to be nervous about."

"Well for starters, my mom kicked me out last time I saw her."

"You never told me that. So you're technically homeless now, like me."

"Technically. Then there's that part where I have never brought a guy home before. Let's hope my mother behaves!"

We pulled into the driveway. I shivered inwardly at how ugly the house was, white house with peach colored shutters and matching colored door. The inside of the house wasn't much better because my mother never had any money to keep up with the maintenance.

"Here goes," I said, taking Jack's hand and heading up to the front step. I opened the door and we walked inside.

"Mom," I called.

"Hi sweetie! Dinner just came out," I heard my mother say. We made our way into the kitchen.

"Mom, this is Jack. Jack, this is my mother, Kathryn."

"So are you the one whisking my daughter away overseas?"

Jack looked at my mother confused.

"Not at all. Jack has actually asked me to stay," I said, annoyed that my mother would try to pick a fight with Jack within a minute of meeting him.

"Oh. I have to admit, I was quite surprised when Clara Kate mentioned she wanted to bring her boyfriend home. I always thought she was a lesbian. You are the first guy I've ever heard her mention."

I looked at Jack who was smiling, probably about me calling him my boyfriend to my mother. I just wanted to see what it felt like rolling that word off my tongue. I quite enjoyed it. I can't believe my mother thought I was a lesbian. I quickly tried to change the conversation.

"So did you find someone to rent my room?"

"Oh you know I'd never throw your things away, honey. I'd like you to be the one to clean out your room."

"Why don't you just charge Thomas rent?"

"I heard that!" I heard Thomas say from his bedroom. I shook my head at my mother.

"He goes to college! You know this."

"College kids pay dorm fees, Mom. Maybe if Thomas got a job," I whispered. My mother gave me the look, the shut the hell up look. So I did.

We made it through dinner without any incident. My mother asked Jack many questions, but their conversation flowed successfully.

I listened as I let him answer all of her questions about how we met and if he was going to travel with me. I loved listening to his voice.

"Do you want to see my bedroom?" I asked, excusing myself from the table and thanking my mother for a wonderful meal.

"Sure."

Jack followed me to my bedroom. I flipped on the light and looked around. It looked exactly how I had left it months ago.

"So you heard your mom. She'd like you to pack up your room."

"I don't want any of this crap."

"This picture of you and Jesse," he said, pointing to a picture on my dresser, "you just want to throw that away?"

"No, but I can't take it all with me."

"I'll store it for you."

I let out a laugh. "You don't even have a place to put your own stuff!"

"Look at all these pictures and memories. I just can't see you throwing them away. This way maybe I'll see you again someday."

"I'll go grab one bag and fill it up with my most prized possessions. Then, I'll donate or discard the rest. Okay?"

"I guess."

I left Jack and headed down the hall to the kitchen where I found my mother cleaning up.

"Do you need any help?" I asked her.

"Not at all, but thank you sweetie."

"Do you have a bag or a box of some sort? I'm just going to put some of my stuff in it and get rid of the rest."

"Oh okay. Here, your brother ordered something online and this package came in the mail. He doesn't need the box though."

"Perfect! Thank you."

"Jack is adorable and so polite. I think you found yourself a real winner!"

Don't I know it.

"Thanks," I said, heading back to my room.

I started making a pile on my bed of all my clothes. I pulled clothes out of my dresser and Jack began taking clothes off the hangers in the closet.

"This is getting real," I said. "I'm never coming back now." Jack looked sad.

"Don't give me that look. I'll be back to visit. You can introduce me to your wife and children."

"I don't know how you can say that like it's nothing. If I came to visit you and you introduced me to your husband and kids, I'd be really sad."

"I know. I'm sorry. I'm just trying to hide the way I feel. I'm going to miss you so much; so much more than you know."

"What's your plan for after?"

"I think I'll house sit until I find somewhere I fall in love with and have enough money to settle down."

"Over there?"

"Yeah."

"What about Jesse and your family? You won't miss them at all?"

"Of course I will," I said, sitting on Jack's lap and kissing him on the cheek. "Look at this place, though. I feel like I'm in a dungeon," I whispered.

"Your mom's house isn't who you are or what your life will be like. If you want a nice house, then I can give you that."

"It's not what I want. I can't see you buying a house and me house sitting around here, never sleeping in the same bed."

"Then don't house sit. You'll find a job."

"I love house sitting, though. Why not house sit from one country to another so I can see the world? I'm not ready to settle down like you..."

"Okay, sorry," he said, seeing I was getting flustered.

"It's okay. It's just...this is the only way I can make money while experiencing the world, at the same time figuring out what I want to do with the rest of my life."

"Is this yours?" Jack asked, plucking a shirt off the pile of clothes.

"Yes. Why?"

"It's huge!"

"I told you I gained weight."

"You said fifty pounds..."

"Okay...so I gained a lot more. Like, a lot a lot! I'm lucky Jesse stayed friends with me. Everyone would whisper behind my back and call me names, but I could hear them. I never disagreed with them either. I was fat and depressed!"

"Wow. I can't even picture it. Do you have any photos of the fat and depressed Clara Kate you speak of?"

"Heck no, but speaking of which, will you pull all of these pictures out of their frames while I clean out my desk?"

"Sure."

I went around my room, grabbing all my frames and leaving them on the bed next to Jack. Then I started opening up my desk drawers and pulling out the contents.

"Hey...who are all these people?" Jack asked.

I took the picture from Jack's hand, squinting my eyes to see all the faces in the picture.

"I don't really know. These are my cousins...I kind of remember them. These three are me and my two brothers. That's why I kept this picture...see we are all crying? I guess we wanted a popsicle and my mother told us we had to wait until after the picture was taken. She probably didn't want us to get our clothes all messy. I wonder what it was like to hear all three of your children crying at the same time," I chuckled.

"Ungodly," Jack said, taking the picture back and looking at it again.

"That guy right there...he looks a lot like the man."

"Yeah, I guess."

"But you don't know him."

"No. This was some family reunion my mother took us to. For all I know, that man could be my father."

"How's it going in here?" my mother asked, stopping in the doorway. "Oh wow, making some progress."

"Yeah. Hey, mom, what's this picture all about?"

"That was a family reunion when you were all just babies."

"I don't see anyone from our family, though."

"That's because it was your father's side. Where did you get this from anyway?"

"I think you threw them out or was going to, so I took it. I just liked that all of us were crying."

"Yeah because I wouldn't let you have a popsicle."

"I remember. Well, I was too young to remember, but you told me when I was a little girl. So, is my father in this picture?" I asked, holding my breath. Surely, she wouldn't get upset with my question in front of Jack.

"Let me see it," she said, extending her hand to take the picture from Jack.

"He is...right here," she said, pointing to a man on the far right of the photograph.

"Wow. I remembered he was tall and skinny, but nothing else. When did I see him last?"

"You already know the answer Clara Kate, you were five!"

"Sorry. It's just...why did he leave?"

"I don't want to have this conversation with you in front of our guest."

Jack got up off my bed and left the room. *Wow. Thank you, Jack*! Now more than ever I wanted to learn about my father.

"What happened?" I asked, sitting on the bed. "I mean, I'm an adult now, so you can tell me."

I looked at the picture again. He did look just like the man, but it wasn't. He didn't have the mustache.

"Did Dad have a brother?"

"He did."

"With a jet black mustache?"

My mother placed her hand over her mouth and started to cry.

Oh no.

"What is it Mom?"

"I told him if he stayed away from you, from all of us, then I wouldn't turn them in. Your father listened. Your uncle on the other hand showed up here out of the blue. He was drunk or messed up on something, but he came looking for you. I told him you were camping in St. Louis and you weren't home. He pushed his way through and had me up against the wall until he saw your brothers were home. Then he walked right out and I never saw him again."

"What was his name?"

"He found you, didn't he?" she asked, ignoring my question.

"What was his name, Mom?"

"Michael...Michael Chassidy. Why?"

"Jack," I called.

"Yeah."

"What was the man's name?" I hollered. Jack appeared in my doorway. He nodded his head.

"Michael Chassidy," Jack confirmed.

"He raped me, Mom. He came to the campground and he raped me. I went with Jesse's family and you had to come pick me up."

The coloring in her face disappeared. Jack noticed the panicked look on my face and ran to my mother.

"Just breathe," he said to her, kneeling down by her side.

"You sent him right to me. What in the world did he FUCKING want from me?" I screamed, tired of her dancing around the truth.

"YOU! He always wanted you!"

"I don't understand," I cried, leaning against the desk and placing my face in my hands.

Why was this happening?

All of a sudden I felt a warm arm around my neck. When I looked over, I saw my brother.

"You knew?" I choked.

"Kind of. I was so young. He had this fascination with you and then it turned into this obsession."

"Can one of you just start from the beginning? And how does everyone manage to know this BUT me?" I asked, completely irritated by how vague they were being.

"Well Dad worked during the day, Clara Kate," Thomas began. "And sometimes he would get home late, so Uncle Mike would always watch us if that happened. That's how it started, but then Uncle Mike would just start hanging around here," he looked to my mother for confirmation and she nodded her head.

"I started noticing your underwear would be on backwards after he watched you," my mother said.

"And I told Mom how he would take you into Mom and Dad's room and lock the door."

"So what did you do?" I asked my mother.

"One day I told Mike I was late to work and hurried out the door. I drove around for ten minutes and when I came back, I unlocked the front door and found the boys playing in their room, but you and Uncle Mike were missing. My bedroom door was locked so I knocked on it. Mike told me to beat it, thinking I was the boys, so I knocked again. He whipped the door open and I caught him by surprise. I weaseled my way through the wedge in the door and found you on the bed completely naked," my mother said, starting to cry. "I completely lost it. I noticed this camera on the bed, so I snatched it and Mike came after me. I tried with all my might to keep him from getting it, but he was so much stronger than me. I screamed and I cussed and he ran out of the house."

"So then what?"

"When your father got home, I told him all about it. I told him we needed to go to the police."

"And?"

"He didn't believe me. He defended him! He told me you were probably naked because you spilled something on yourself and had to be changed. I was outraged! You can't imagine how a mother feels when she finds her little girl is being sexually abused."

"But you don't know that, Mom."

"The camera...the locked door. C'mon, Clara Kate. The wool was pulled over my eyes too. Mike was one of my favorite people, but he'd never bring any girlfriends around. Anywhere we went...the fair or just out in general, he would stop and admire the young girls. It took a while for me to make the connection," she said, shaking her head and squeezing at the bridge of her nose.

"Can we get to the part where Dad left?"

"I went to work one night and the next morning you kids told me Uncle Mike stopped by. Your father denied it. He wouldn't even confront him, but then he had the nerve to let him come inside our house? I don't care if he was his brother, I would beat the living daylights out of anyone who harmed my children. HE LET HIM IN OUR HOUSE! They're a disgrace...the both of them."

"So you kicked him out?"

"I talked about moving and not telling anyone where we went. Your father didn't want that. I always felt vulnerable after that. Every time I went to work, all I could think about was if Mike was there with you. I couldn't do it anymore. I gave your father an ultimatum and he chose his brother. Who knows, maybe he was into the same thing too."

"This is so messed up..." I said, pacing the room.

"I know. I'm so sorry, sweetheart."

"Is that why you drove me to school every day?"

"Until high school, yes."

"That's why you worked from home?"

"Until you went to high school and I felt like you were old enough to start giving you more freedom. I never would've thought he would come find you."

"You told him where I was!"

"Jesse's family vacationed at that campground every year! Mike knew Jesse's parents before you two even became friends!"

"You led him right to me! Why? Why'd he do it? And why after all those years did he come looking for me?"

"I HAVE NO CLUE, CLARA KATE! He was REALLY sick in the head!"

"So he broke our family up?"

"Your father broke our family up. He could've turned his brother in. At the very least he should've told Mike never to come back here."

"Wait, why isn't my last name Chassidy then?"

"Your father and I never got married."

"Why?"

"I don't really know. We talked about it...I mean, we were engaged, but we started a family and just never made it to the altar."

"Wow. So I have your last name..."

"Yes."

"I just can't believe I didn't know any of this. Did you know we had mom's last name?" I asked, looking at my brother. He shook his head. I can't believe I never thought to ask. I just assumed I had my father's last name.

"So Dad didn't care about us? He never tried to see us on our birthdays or anything?"

"Oh no, he did. He would show up here late at night after you kids were asleep and tell me he was going to take custody of you. I remember being so afraid, but I'd never let him know it."

"But he never did?"

"I threatened child support. He was making really good money in the military; he was high up in the ranks. I also told him I would go to the police about Mike and tell them he was in on it too. I had no evidence, but I guess your father fell for it because he stopped showing up."

"Where is he now?"

"I have no idea, honey."

I looked at Jack. *Jack could find him. Did I want to know where he was?* I didn't know...we all sat there in silence for a moment. Jack made his way over to me, putting his hand on my shoulder.

"We can finish cleaning your room another night," he said, quietly.

"I got everything I wanted," I said, my voice shaking. "How do you want me to get rid of the rest?" I asked my mother.

"I'll bag it all and donate it. You know, just because I need to rent your room out doesn't mean you can't call this home."

"I know," I lied. From as far back as I could remember, I never wanted to call this place home. Maybe now I knew why.

"Are you going to be okay?" my mother asked. "I know this is a lot of information for you to process."

"I guess. I haven't really wrapped my head around it. I think I'm going to go if that's okay."

"Sure," my mother said, standing from the bed to come hug me.

"Thanks for dinner."

"Anytime. I love you sweetie. Please come say goodbye right before you leave. You are coming back, aren't you?"

"Oh yeah. I just want to see the world for a little while and then I'll be home."

"Nice meeting you," my mother said to Jack, giving him a hug.

"What's his name, Mom?"

"Whose name?"

"My father's."

"Ray," she said softly, with tears in her eyes almost like it hurt to even say his name. I turned to my brother.

"Bye," I said, and he gave me a sideways hug. I can't remember the last time we had shown one another any sort of affection. It was nice...just really weird.

I felt like I could breathe again once we were out of the house and on our way towards the car. When we got inside Jack's car, he turned to me.

"What the hell was all that about?"

"I have no flipping clue!"

"You're coming back home? That's not what you told me."

"I lied. If I didn't, she would try to stop me."

Jack turned the car on, placing it in drive and pulled out of the driveway.

"And why didn't she even ask you about the rape? You literally just told her your uncle raped you and she had no questions. She didn't want to know anything..."

"Yeah. I mean, what happened to me was the reason she and I butted heads throughout my entire high school career. Do you think she had some sort of inclination to my grades slipping and weight gain? He shows up at our house while I'm camping and I come home sick the next day. C'mon..."

"She had to have told him where you were. Maybe he threatened her."

"You heard her. My uncle knew Jesse's family. Anyone and everyone who knows Jesse's family knows they go to the same campgrounds on the same weekends every year."

"I don't like anything about that story she just told you."

"Why? I mean, she kicked my dad out. That was pretty courageous raising three kids on her own just to protect one of them."

I looked over to Jack who was shaking his head.

"You don't believe anything she said?"

"No."

"I'll call my oldest brother, maybe he remembers something."

I curled up into a fetal position and faced my body away from Jack.

"Hey, what's going on?" he asked, placing his hand on my thigh.

I started to bawl my eyes out. I just wanted to run away and never come back...far away from everyone.

"Clara Kate, stop trying to be so brave. What happened to you was really messed up, but I promise you, it's never going to happen to you again."

"How do you know that?"

"Because you're getting far away from here."

"I wish I could just leave today. I'm not ever going back there..."

After a few minutes of silence, we were home. Jack parked his car and shut it off.

"I'll finish up your house sitting job here if you really want to leave here tonight."

I opened the door and slammed it shut, stomping up to the house and unlocking the door.

"What? What did I say?" Jack asked.

"I literally have nobody except you and it's obvious you don't give a shit if I just pack my bags and take the next flight out tonight."

"What? No, no, no! Don't put thoughts into your head that aren't realistic. Sometimes I feel like I care about you more than anybody."

Not good enough! I stomped to the bedroom, whipping my purse at the wall and jumping onto the bed. I wanted to scream!

"Clara Kate, you're being ridiculous! I have no fucking clue what's going through your mind right now. You know I don't want you to go, but if I were you, I wouldn't want to stay either and since I love you, I will help you any way that I can. You yourself mentioned leaving this very day and I just offered to make that happen."

"Why are you here?" I sat up, looking at Jack. He had absolutely nothing to say. "You know I'm going, so what makes you stay?"

"You."

"You just need somewhere to stay?"

"It was your idea for me to move in here with you!"

"Well, I think you should move out!" I said, closing my eyes. I was too weak to even see the pain I knew he'd have in his eyes.

"Fine!" he growled. He picked up the box of my belongings I had just emptied from my room and discarded them onto the floor. Then he began throwing his stuff into the box. I laid down and sobbed. *Why was I pushing him away?* This wasn't what I wanted. My cries clawed at my own heart. I craved a normal life. I just wanted a functional relationship.

When Jack was through, I heard him pick up the box and leave. Moments later he climbed into bed next to me and wrapped his arms around me. I cried even harder. He squeezed me so tight it almost hurt. After a couple minutes he loosened his grip and held me until I fell asleep.

****

I woke up and rolled over to an empty bed. I jumped up and walked around the house, but there was no sign of Jack. *Shoot*! Just then the front door opened and in walked Jack and Rocky.

"Morning," he said.

"Hey...I thought you left."

"Rocky woke me up whining, so I took him for a walk."

"Thank you. You didn't have to do that."

I watched Jack take Rocky's leash off and discard it on top of Rocky's cage. Then he picked up his box of belongings he had packed from the night before.

"I don't...I don't want you to go," I confessed.

"It doesn't matter."

"It does to me."

"Why?"

"Because I'm so messed up right now and you're the only one that makes me want to keep going."

He sat on the couch and I went to him, sitting in his lap. I wrapped my arms around his neck and placed my head on his chest.

"You keep pushing me away," he whispered.

"I know. I don't know why. I can't promise you that I won't do it again, but please just stay with me."

I heard Jack let out a sigh. *Oh no, I ruined it this time.*

"Are you hungry?" he asked. I couldn't help but smile. Maybe this means he's staying.

"For you," I said, getting off Jack's lap and kneeling in front of him. Maybe this was my way of saying sorry or the only way I could think to get him to stay, but there was something about having an argument that really turned me on.

I pulled at Jack's shorts, doing the only intimate thing I was really good at. I desperately needed to feel close to him again. Jack was hesitant at first, but the more I licked and sucked, the harder he got. I smiled at him when I was finished and he tried to hide his grin.

"You didn't have to do that," he said.

"I know. I was a really big jerk last night and I'm sorry. Does that make up for it?"

"Definitely," he said, grabbing me abruptly and placing me back in his lap. "I love you so much it hurts. I feel helpless knowing somebody hurt you...that's what I do for a living, protect people."

"But the damage has already been done."

"I know..."

"I'll be okay, Jack."

"Gaining weight and insomnia okay?"

"No. Please don't think I am crazy, but I think I want to face this...all of it. I want to go see my uncle. Maybe he holds all my answers..."

"Clara Kate, you blacked out just seeing a photo of the guy. I don't think that's a good idea."

"Can you get a picture of him again?"

"Of course."

"Could you find out where he's being held?"

"I could."

"Will you do that for me?"

He shook his head.

"Please?"

"I'm telling you right now this has bad idea written all over it." He looked away and then back into my eyes, searching for the answer. "But for you, I'll do it."

"I'm tired of living in the dark and being afraid. I want to march in there and demand the truth…once and for all."

Jack let out a loud sigh. Then he picked me up and disposed of me on the couch before exiting the room. I think this new idea of mine was testing his patience. Moments later, I walked past him in the kitchen and out onto the back deck to take care of the chickens. When I was finished, I went to clean the litter box. After I washed my hands, I found Jack at the table with two plates full of waffles, sausages and bacon.

"Orange juice?" he asked.

"Please. You know, you really are perfect."

"Far from it. Just because I don't talk about my pain, it doesn't mean I don't feel any. I'm okay now with the whole Jezebel thing. When you first met me I was a mess, but I've come to realize it just wasn't meant to be. Jamison though, I wonder if the pain of losing your own child ever goes away. I mean, does it get better when you have another child? Will those sad emotions then be replaced with happier ones?"

"I don't know. How many children do you want?"

"At least a couple. I was an only child and I hated it. I was so lonely growing up."

"Weren't you spoiled?"

"Yeah, with toys I had to play with all by myself."

"Good point. I miss my Maddy, but I try not to think about it. Is that wrong?"

"Really? There's not a day that goes by that I don't think of Jamison."

I sat there eating my breakfast and sneaking every glance I could at Jack. It was during moments like this I wondered how I was ever going to leave. I had a thousand reasons to leave Missouri, but here I am, sitting across from the one reason I wanted to stay.

"You're in deep thought," he said, snapping me back into focus.

"I have to go find my next house job. Today! I can't keep putting it off."

"How long are you looking for?"

"There's a lot of one month or three-month jobs and then it skips until a whole year. I was hoping for something that's around six weeks. One month sounds too short and three is too long if I don't like the house or if I just want to come back home."

"To me."

"Yes. I'm not ever going back to my mother's house; I can promise you that. Besides, Jesse said I could stay at her parent's house. They're like my second family."

"You never talk about Jesse anymore."

"I know. My teachers warned us about this before we graduated, that we would drift apart from all our friends and find new ones. I just didn't think it was going to happen this fast. The worst part is, I don't miss her the way I know I should. She probably feels the same way. I was always bringing her down because I never wanted to go out with her friends...my old friends."

"I'm surprised she didn't understand after she found out..."

"No, she did. Jesse is a great friend. She's been there for me through everything. It's just, the older I got the more I realized we had less in common. I realized it even more after I met you. She's slept with at least thirty guys and who knows how many different guys she's given blow jobs to. After everything you and I have done, I don't understand how she just gets up the next morning and does it all over again with a different guy."

"Yeah...I never understood that either. Jamison's mother kind of ruined the whole sex thing for me or maybe I would've had sex with more than just two people. I was busy trying to become a police officer and be a father to Jamison, but I had a couple girls who were interested in me and just knowing I could impregnate them made me run away."

I started giggling.

"So I'm not the only one with a fear of sex," I laughed.

"I'm okay now. Once I had a stable job and matured a bit, I was fine."

"Would you ever try having sex with me again?" I asked, holding my breath.

"I don't know. Why?"

"Just wondering. I'm not ready, but someday I hope I am. After that I want to try having sex in the shower. These are my sex goals."

I heard Jack let out a chuckle.

"I'm going to go shower," he said, getting up and bringing his plate to the sink. I sat at the table, scrolling through the new house sitting jobs that were posted that day. I clicked on the first one and started reading it when the doorbell rang. I jumped, knowing it wasn't Jack.

"Hi," Jezebel said, with a big smile on her face. She was wearing a tight-fitting dress that revealed a lot of cleavage. *Holy boobs!* There were tiny slits all the way down the sides of her dress, revealing her skin. *Damn was she gorgeous!*

"H...hello," I stuttered.

"Is Jack here?" she asked, nodding in the direction of his car parked in the driveway.

"Ummm...yes...well, no." *Why was I so nervous around her?* "He's showering."

"Oh, okay. Will you please tell him I stopped by? Actually, you can just tell him...I can officially buy out his half of our house. My grandfather is going to give me the money up front and let me pay him back in installments."

"That's great!"

"Yes, it really is."

I felt like Jezebel should be mean to me. I mean, I am the next woman, but here she was still pleasantly smiling.

"I hope you know how lucky you are," she said. I stood there unsure of what to say. "Every time I've asked about you it's like he just comes alive. I've never seen him like that and I hope you appreciate him more than I did."

I smiled, at a loss for words.

"Bye," she said, turning around and walking back down the walkway. *How the hell did she walk in those killer heels? And she made it look easy!*

"Bye." I quickly went inside and straight to the bathroom, eager to tell Jack the good news. I knocked on the door.

"Yeah?"

"Can I come in?"

"Yeah, babe." I opened the door, my face hit by the steam from the hot water. "You okay?"

"Yeah. Jezebel just stopped by," I said, quickly undressing and tossing my clothes aside on the floor.

"Oh jeez."

"Well how'd she know where to find you?"

"I told her I was staying the street over. She probably saw my car. What'd she want?"

"She has some good news," I said, drawing back the shower curtain and hopping inside. Jack jumped.

"You just scared the shit out of me," he said. I couldn't help but laugh.

"Sorry. I thought we should start conserving water."

"Yeah…sure you do. What are you up to now? You know, last time you came in here while I was showering you took me by surprise too."

"I remember. So Jezebel has the money to buy you out. She said her grandfather is loaning it to her."

"Did she say how much?"

"No. Why?"

"I told her I wanted half of the value of the home. She thought she was just going to give me half of what we owed."

"Half of what you owe sounds fair."

"Not at all. We bought our house right after the market crashed and now the price of houses has been on the rise. Not to mention all the work I put into it. I paid to have it assessed and told her to pay half of that value instead."

"You drive a tough bargain!"

"Yeah right, it's the least she could do."

"She seems really nice."

"Yeah…she fooled me too."

I rolled my eyes at Jack, not wanting to talk about Jezebel anymore. I leaned towards him, grabbing his waist and bringing his body flush with mine.

"What's going on in that head of yours?" he asked.

"I want to be with you…right here…right now."

"Clara Kate, you yourself said…"

"I know what I said, but I want this. This is my choice and I can't think of a better guy to do it with. Please?"

Jack put his forehead against mine and closed his eyes.

"Just go slow," I whispered.

"Even if I wanted to…I don't have any condoms."

"You do want to," I said, looking down at his erection. "We don't need a condom; Jesse has told me countless times she uses the pull-out method and she's never gotten pregnant."

"If you got pregnant, would that make you stay?" he asked.

"If I got pregnant, would that make you come with me?"

"You always have me second guessing myself," he said, kissing me on my lips. He trailed kisses across my cheek and down to my neck.

"You are the reason I no longer second guess myself," I said, anticipating Jack's next move. He kissed his way down my chest, taking my breast, one by one into his mouth and teasing each nipple. He licked and sucked until I couldn't take it anymore.

"Jack," I breathed. I lifted my leg and wrapped it around his waist, digging my heel into his butt and pulling him tighter against me. He grabbed his cock, rubbing it at my entrance and slowly made his way inside. The feeling was exquisite as he softly rocked back and forth inside me. In a sex slated trance, I began to moan. Jack looked at me and I grabbed his face, bringing his lips to mine. This time I made my way inside his mouth with my tongue. He sucked at my lip and I could feel my orgasm start to build.

"Oh fuck," Jack said, panting and that was enough for me to let go. Jack pulled out. I dropped to my knees and caught his semen in my mouth.

"What the heck?" he asked, surprised.

"What?" I stood back up, looking at Jack who had a big smile on his face.

"Why did you just do that?"

"Sorry...I just saw the girls doing it in those porn videos Jesse and I used to watch."

"That was literally the sexiest thing I have every witnessed. Just hearing you moan was enough for me, but holy shit! I mean, I could've just cum down the drain..."

"Oh, okay..."

"No...please. If that's what you want to do then by all means..."

I shrugged my shoulders. Jack brought me to him, wrapping his arms around my neck and letting the hot water cascade over us.

"You are un-fucking-believable. Everything about you. I swear I fall in love with you more and more each day."

"Me too." *I just had sex! I JUST HAD SEX! IN THE SHOWER! Was I cured?* I wasn't sure. This was a major stepping stone! "Was slow paced sex okay?" I asked.

"Forget about me, what about you? How are you feeling?"

"So alive! I surprise myself, Jack. But seriously, was I okay?"

"Yeah. I'm not going to lie, I've never had sex like that before, but I was so turned on. It was like a slow torture, but so fucking hot. I was craving the need to go faster and you denying me that gave me such a high."

"Maybe someday you can show me your favorite way to have sex," I said.

"I don't know…I liked whatever we just did a hell of a lot."

"I hope you don't feel used. I…"

Jack put his finger over my lips to silence me.

"I already apologized for that. I'm sorry I ever said it. You're giving me a part of yourself you've never given anyone and I feel beyond privileged for that."

****

Now here I was, holding the answers to all my questions. Michael Chassidy, Boone County Jail, serving forty years behind bars.

"Forty years for aggravated and statutory rape," I said, as Jack watched me read the piece of paper he left for me the night before.

"That's a serious conviction."

"Not serious enough. We'll both still be alive when he's released."

"God willing."

"This is crazy," I said, still staring at the information.

"What?"

"I just never imagined I would learn who raped me…let alone given the chance to ask him why."

"Prisoners have rights. He may deny your visit."

"Really?"

"He probably will."

"Can I drive you to work and I'll take your car to go see him?"

"Boone County has visitation rules. I already looked into them. It goes by first letter of last name, C falls on Tuesdays."

"That's today!" I exclaimed.

"I know, but we're too late. Visitation for males starts at eight-thirty and ends one hour later. I'm sorry, Clara Kate..."

"And that's it?"

"Evenings start at eight-thirty for one hour long too."

"So I'll drop you off and go," I suggested.

"First of all, I have to make a phone call and try to get you on the contact list. Then I have to see if I can get next Tuesday off so I can go with you."

"I can't wait that long."

"Clara Kate, you're not going by yourself and that's all there is to it."

Jack was treating me like a child and I hated it. I just wanted to be done with this so I could move on and never look back. So many questions remained. *Why did Michael come looking for me that night? How did he find me at the campground? Where is my father?*

"Fine," I said, chock full of attitude. "But we leave bright and early next Tuesday morning!" Jack just smiled at me in amusement.

During the week I did a lot of research for my next house sitting job. I wouldn't have a vehicle, so I would need to be in a city setting. I narrowed it down to London and Paris, for starters. Then I would keep my eye out in hopes I could visit Greece, Ireland, Germany, Spain and Portugal. I was so excited! I wouldn't stop there; I would travel to every place I could. As long as I was making money in order to start a life when I was ready to settle down, then I was all in!

"Morning, baby," I said, rolling over and kissing Jack on his forehead.

"You were out cold when I got home."

"I didn't even hear you. I found my next adventure!"

"Where?"

"London."

"Wow. What's in London?"

"I have no clue, but it looks amazing!"

"There's pictures of the house?"

"Well no. The house sounds kind of small. I didn't get to see pictures actually."

"Why did you take the job then?"

"Well, it's within walking distance to everything I want to see and I've never done anything like this before. The guy owns a book club and he needs someone to fill in for him while he is gone, which is for eight weeks."

"Wow."

"I know. He'll actually be in the United States while I'm there, but he didn't say why. Anyway, I'll be sending out books and processing books that get returned as well. It all sounds pretty easy to me."

"I think you're brilliant!"

"Why?"

"You have eight weeks to not only get an impression, but to leave one as well. Then you can pack up and do it all over again elsewhere. I've never met anyone like you."

"Ditto," I said, leaning over and kissing him. "You are one of a kind!"

"So when are you leaving?" he asked.

"You have me for three more weeks...twenty-one days. I'll need to find a hotel once I get to London because the man doesn't need me until the end of the week. It'll be fine, though. I'm really excited!"

"Stay here with me then until you have to start there."

"With you and Jezebel? Yeah right!"

"I hate how you act like it's just so easy to walk away."

"It's not. You knew this was happening Jack. I made it very clear from the beginning. I can't give up my dreams for you...I won't do it. I literally have nothing here."

"You do too! You just don't realize it."

"My mother's house? You want me to stay there for a few days before I have to leave? For all I know she already found someone to rent my room."

"Just stay...please. I'll rent a hotel room here. I don't care how much it costs!"

"Let's spend the next few weeks looking for a house for you and if you find one, I'll stay there with you until I leave. Okay?"

"It takes months for a bank to approve a loan. You just don't get it, do you?" he growled and left the room. Jack was the last person I wanted to be upset with me. I didn't even know what I did wrong.

For the rest of the week, Jack was really distant. There were two days I hardly even saw him. He was at Jezebel's packing his belongings. He even went to his aunt's house after work a few times. This was the last thing I wanted, for Jack and me to spend the end of our time together apart because he was upset I was leaving.

I wasn't trying to make him feel insignificant. In fact, he was the most important person in my life right now. I think deep down he thought he was going to get me to stay and now that he realized I was following through with my plan, he had to push me away to safeguard his heart. I let him. I was always the one to make the first move when I wanted to be intimate, but I fought the urge. When I felt him climb into bed at night, I wouldn't even roll over to say hello. I, too, started to feel like I should safeguard my own heart.

By the time Tuesday morning rolled around, I was ready to get the show on the road. I pictured having to drag Jack to the car rubbing his sleepy eyes from working the night before, but he was ready and waiting when I got out of the shower. I was beyond appreciative he remembered today.

"There's really no reason to do this," he said, when we climbed into his car.

"I just want to know why. Maybe then I can get on with my life and stop living in the past."

"I know why. He's sick, Clara Kate. I see guys like him all the time who prey on young girls."

"But why come looking for ME, Jack?"

"Okay," he said, patient as ever.

It took an hour to get there. I was a terrible co-pilot, unable to form a sentence, let alone hold a conversation. I had a thousand questions flowing through my brain. I tried to picture Michael's face the entire car ride there so there would be no surprises when I saw him...if I saw him. I would be so upset if he denied my visit. It's not like he would hear my name and not know who I was.

"How old is Michael Chassidy?"

"I can find out for you," Jack replied.

I don't know why, but there was something inside of me that wanted to know everything about him. *What was his life like growing up?* I know my grandparents died in a car accident during a terrible snowstorm. I remember my mother telling me my father was young at the time. *How old was Michael? Did he go to college?*

"How long can I talk to him for?"

"One hour. I'm starting to think you're obsessing over this."

Me too.

When we arrived, Jack got out of his car.

"You can wait for me here," I suggested.

"I'll just walk you inside. Are you okay?"

No.

"I think so," I lied, looking around. The building was made out of brick. It wasn't very tall, but it was massive in length. I saw the chain link fence with barbed wire coils at the top, which caused a giant wave of nerves to crash over me.

"You'll have to leave your purse in the car. Take your license...it's just easier."

"Why?"

"So they have nothing to search. You can't have any cellphones, cameras, recording devices..."

"Okay, okay...I get it," I said, throwing my purse into the car. I hated rules and I was still frustrated by Jack continuing to be distant. He didn't even hold my hand in the car. He always held my hand!

Jack held the door open for me and I stood outside, hesitating. My biggest fear was the unknown. I needed to know what was about to happen and not having that control was debilitating to my mind.

"You'll need to complete this visitor's application," a man said, handing me a clipboard with paperwork. I turned around to see Jack sitting in a chair behind me. *I don't even remember walking through that door.*

I sat next to Jack staring at the paperwork. *First name...first name...first name.* My hand was shaking. I looked over at Jack wanting him to say something to calm my nerves, but he didn't. He leaned over and kissed my hair. *Maybe he was right...this was a bad idea.*

"Will he be able to touch me?" I whispered in Jack's ear while I waited.

"There's usually a no touching policy."

"But he can break the rules and touch me?"

"Are you asking if it's a face-to-face contact, Clara Kate? I don't know. Listen..."

"No. I'm okay. I was just wondering what to expect."

Jack sighed heavily and looked away.

"Clara Kate." I snapped my head in the direction of my name being called by a tall black lanky man. He ordered me to walk through the metal detector, to which I obliged. I followed him down this long hallway, passing people sitting in a chair talking to their imprisoned love one on the other side of the glass. *Phew*! *Michael couldn't touch me*. Everyone had a phone to their ear.

The guard stopped abruptly and I squeezed by him to sit down. There was no one on the other side. The guard left me in my trance of utter fear. I flung my arms up onto the small table and sobbed into my hands. I was scared. I was so scared! I lifted my head before I fell into a state of hyperventilating that I couldn't climb my way out of and there he was. The man. I stared at him and he stared back at me. After a moment I wondered how long this would go on for, but I couldn't move. It was almost like I was frozen. I didn't have a single word I could think to say.

That mustache. The jet black one that haunted me was the same. He rose out of his chair and leaned in towards me. I jumped back in a frenzy. He stuck his nose to the glass, his cuffed hands dangling in front of him and started to draw something...letters...S...O...R...R...

A guard grabbed him by the back of his shirt and yanked him backward. I jumped out of my chair and pressed my face to the glass to see what was going on. Michael didn't put up a fight as the guard hauled him away. He never tried to look back. I sat back down in my chair, my chest heaving. He said nothing. I said nothing. And now he was gone.

When I finally found the strength in my legs, I was out of there. I quickly walked towards the entrance of the building, past Jack who was still sitting by the door.

"What happened?" he demanded, following me out into the parking lot.

"Nothing!" I grumbled.

"Doesn't look like nothing to me. What did he say?"

With my hands on my hips, I snapped. "Hmmm...let me think if there is another way to say it..." I was chock full of attitude. "He said absolutely nothing." I stood at the passenger side of Jack's car and waited until I heard the beep beep that unlocked my door. I climbed in and dialed the only person that may still hold all my answers.

"Clara Kate," my brother sang through the line.

"Tyler," I cried, not knowing where I was even going to begin.

"Woah, woah. What's going on? Are you okay?"

"Michael...Uncle Mike. Do you remember him?"

"Sure I do."

"What did he do to me? Please tell me why Dad left!"

"What happened, Clara Kate?"

"I went to visit Michael in jail."

"Jesus. What for? Stay the fuck away from him!"

"Why?"

"He's all sorts of messed up!"

"How do you know?"

I heard Tyler on the other line taking a deep breath in and exhaling. *Please tell me!*

"I hope you don't think I'm crazy and please don't you ever tell Mom this, but I think he and Dad were running some kind of prostitution ring with little girls."

I put my hand up to my mouth. I didn't think I could stomach anymore.

"Do you know where to find Dad?" I asked, changing the subject.

"He's dead, Sis. He died right after Madeline. When I left home, the first thing I did was try to find him. I flew to Colorado once I learned of his passing. Does Mom know you went to visit Uncle Mike?"

"No."

"Good. She's been through enough."

"Why? Why do you say that? I just get this feeling that she's hiding something from me."

"I don't know much because I was so young, but I knew growing up she went to great lengths to protect you. If she's hiding anything it's in your best interest and you better leave well enough alone. Okay?"

"Okay," I said, not wanting to settle the fact that I believed my mother knew more, but knowing I should listen to my brother. He was the best older brother I could ever ask for.

"Some things are better left in the past, you know? Maybe you don't know, but you need to just trust me on this one. Mom loves you and that's all that matters. Are you going to be okay?"

"I think so."

"Call me if you need anything. I love you."

"Okay. I love you, too," I said, hitting the end button and knowing full well I should've asked him how he was making it in Denver. I looked at Jack.

"I'm sorry," he said. I hated when someone apologized for something they didn't do. It was a waste of an apology.

I sat there fuming. Yeah, I talked a good game, thinking I could go in there and rattle off a slew of questions to the man who stole all my teenage years. *How could I just sit there and let the opportunity pass me by? What a waste of time!*

"DAMNIT!" I yelled, punching Jack's dashboard.

Ow, my hand. Why did I just do that?

"What the hell happened in there? Just tell me!"

I sat there consumed by all these dreaded thoughts of rape and now prostitution. The further I went digging for information, the more I wondered if I was ever going to make it out of this dark hole.

"I'm here for you," Jack said, placing his hand on my knee.

"Here for me? I've barely seen you all week! You've been at your aunt's and hanging out with Jezebel!"

"She's not even home this week! She's in Europe for fashion week. Hey...maybe you two can meet up and become friends...swap stories about the size of my penis."

I looked over at him. He wasn't smiling. He was serious. I frivolously grabbed at the handle in an attempt to open the car door, but it was locked. I undid my seatbelt and unlocked the door.

"What are you doing?" Jack shouted, as I opened the door. He slowed down just enough for me to jump out. We were on a dirt road and there were no cars or houses in sight.

"Are you fucking mental?" he yelled, stopping his car and getting out.

"I've had it with you! I'm not getting back in that car. You're such an asshole!"

"Just tell me what I did? Why are you so mad at me?"

"Why are you so distant with me? We've hardly talked all week!"

"What does it matter? YOU'RE LEAVING!" he screamed, exacerbated.

"It does matter! I have just a couple of weeks left and we're spending it like this?" I screamed back.

"I'm pissed off. I have to start all over again with a new house and a new girl."

"It doesn't matter! You're still so young! Stop planning every minute of your fucking life and just live it!"

"See...that right there...you don't care. You don't give a shit that I am in love with you."

I went to Jack. He was shaking and I had never seen him so angry.

"I do," I said, grabbing his hands. "I swear I do. This is the same conversation again and again, Jack. We can't keep doing this!"

He grabbed my face, catching me off guard and kissed me fiercely. I broke away and dropped to my knees, fumbling with the button on his jeans.

"Clara Kate..." he protested, but before he could say another word, I had him in my mouth. I heard him begin to moan and knew the fight was over. I had to close the distance between us, it was literally killing me. He grabbed my shoulders and brought me to a standing position. Then he whipped me around and bent me over the hood of his car. I quickly undid my pants and pulled them down along with my underwear.

"Fuck!" he growled, slamming both hands down onto his car. The sound of his palms hitting the metal hood made me jump. I stifled a giggle as he made his way inside me. He was pissed off, knowing he could get slapped with indecent exposure at any given minute, but the feeling was too addicting to stop.

Jack was quick and he made it clear this was definitely not for my pleasure as he pulled out of me and discarded his semen onto the side of the road before I could orgasm. I turned and smiled at him. He pulled his pants back up, a heated look on his face as he leaned in close until our noses were touching. I arched back, staring into his eyes as he placed a hand down on the car on either side of me.

"Don't ever do that again," he warned in a low tone. *Uh oh*. He stood back up, glaring at me. My eyes followed his over to his side of the car until he climbed in. *Oh no, he's pissed.* I eagerly climbed inside.

"Sorry," I whispered.

"You could've just cost me my job!"

That's a little dramatic, I thought, as Jack put the car in drive and we headed back home again.

"Can we do it again?" I asked, letting my sexual frustration from not orgasming get the better of me. Jack burst out laughing. *Phew!*

"You're wild!" he smirked.

"In a good way or a bad way?"

"I haven't decided. Either way you completely disarm me. It's a feeling I'm not used to having."

"Sorry."

"No you're not. You probably WOULD do it all over again!" *Yes, I would.* "Maybe even with people around." *No way!* I shot him an evil look. I was a very private person and he knew that.

"What?" he asked.

"You make me this way," I replied, grabbing his hand and kissing it. I sat there looking at his hand interlaced with mine, admiring how safe they made me feel. Jack took his eyes off the road to wrap his arm around me, bringing me to him and kissing me on my head.

"I love you so much," he breathed.

"I love you too. Now eyes on the road so we don't crash!"

"Are you going to tell me what happened?"

"If you tell me why you've been acting so weird this week."

"I'm just sad...what do you want me to say? You know how I feel...I wish you would stay."

"Can we just spend these last two weeks having the time of our lives instead of dwelling on the inevitable?"

"Okay..."

"You promise?"

"I promise. Boy scout honor."

"Oh please, you are anything but a boy scout."

"I was too! I'll have you know I graduated an Eagle and will stay true to my word, giving you the time of your life starting tonight when I bury myself between your legs until you beg me to stop."

"Oh my!" I said. "I'm so sexually frustrated right now and you are not making it any better."

"I know," he said, grinning devilishly at me. *Oh did I love him!*

"So...I saw Michael..." I said, shutting down my libido.

"You did?"

"I panicked! It's like I couldn't find my voice. I totally closed up, Jack!"

"It's okay. That was a huge step just going there, knowing you would be face to face with him."

"He didn't say anything either. We just stared at each other. It was then I thought memories of him would return, but they didn't."

"That's probably best."

"He said he was sorry."

"I thought he didn't talk..."

"He didn't. It was the creepiest thing I've ever witnessed. He put his hot breath on the glass between us. I was just frozen there...I had no idea what the hell he was doing. Then he drew out the word sorry with his nose."

"With his nose?"

"Yeah. What the heck was that about? I don't know. He was handcuffed, but his hands were in front of him. I'm telling you, creepy doesn't even begin to describe it."

"What did he look like?"

"Nothing like that picture you showed me. He's aged a lot."

"Prison will do that to you."

"So he says he's sorry. Sorry for what? For whatever he did when I was a little girl that I can't remember or sorry for raping me when I was fourteen?"

"Maybe all of it," Jack replied.

"I just want to go home, lay in your arms and forget this day ever happened."

"Okay...me too. Well, most of it. I never want to forget bending you over the hood of my car in the middle of the road and having my way with you."

"I knew you enjoyed that! Trying to pretend you're all pissed off at me. It's not like I held a gun to your head."

"You didn't have to. That's what drives me crazy about you. I just do this shit willingly," he said, shaking his head.

"No more fighting?" I asked, kissing his hand again.

"No more fighting."

Jack stayed true to his word when we returned home. I had so many orgasms, I lost count. By the end of the night, I was completely exhausted. I found myself dozing off right after I laid down in Jack's arms.

"Will you write me a letter? One that I won't read until I'm up in the air and on my way to London."

"Okay...but why?" Jack asked.

"I just want something I can always go back to and read, even years later. I still have that note you wrote me and left on the doorstep of your aunt's house. There's something I just loved about that note. It's almost like it stops time because whenever I read it, it feels like I'm right back in that moment."

"So does that mean you will write me one too?" he asked.

"I'm not good at writing."

"What? Me either!"

"Yes you are!"

"Just try it...for me," he pleaded.

"What do you want me to say?"

"Well, I'll tell you how you make me feel so why don't you do the same."

"Okay. I'll give it a shot. Does it have to be long?"

"Clara Kate, you are overthinking this. Just take out a piece of paper and write out your heart. If you feel what you think you do, then it should flow out of you freely."

"I wish I was as good with emotions as you are."

"So, do you want to come house hunting with me?" he asked, changing the subject.

"I'd love to!"

"Okay, I'll have my realtor set up some showings this weekend."

"Do you already have a realtor?"

"It's Jezebel's sister. She found the house we currently live in."

"Oh," I said, wondering if she was anything like Jezebel.

I placed two white lined pieces of paper and two pens on the dining room table when we got home that night.

"What is that for?" he asked.

"A way to stop time. It's for our love letters."

"I'll need way more paper than that!"

"Seriously?" I asked, confused.

"No," he laughed. "I'm joking. Just a few sentences will do."

"Are you messing with me? I need to know so I can write the same amount."

"Stop. Again, you're overthinking this!"

I guess Jack was right because it's been three days and I still haven't come up with a single word to write. Jack's piece of paper and pen were gone the next day. The pressure has been on ever since to sit down and just write how I feel. *This shouldn't be so hard!*

To Jack...

Right now, I'm going to freeze time. I'll write out everything in my head so that every time you read this it will bring you back to that time in your life that you met a girl named Clara Kate.

Let's rewind back to life before Jack Mac. I need you to know me in order to realize your influence on my life was nothing short of a miracle. See, I was detached from the world. I felt like I was living on the outside of myself looking in. Maybe you know what that feels like. You're walking through life unable to see the purpose of anything. Why am I doing it? What is it all for?

I have felt powerless, fearful and have looked over my shoulder every day for the last four years. I have felt used, dirty and ashamed. Every time I met someone new, all I would think about is if they could see right through me. Could they sense I was broken? Did they know I was raped?

I hated cops. The brutal truth is, I hated men in general. Even a high five or a handshake would have my palms sweating with nerves. I ran away from intimacy. I believed sex was a bad thing that men used to gain power. Before I met you, I lived a world of anxiety, flashbacks and panic attacks.

I know what you are thinking right now. Why did I let you in? I pushed you away, Jack, and you didn't go. Then I really pushed you away and you still didn't leave. My mother threatened to send me away and then Jesse threatened to stop being my best friend, but you...you stayed. Oh no, tears have just fallen from my eyes and smudged the ink. Now you know how special you have made me feel...so special I am crying just writing about it.

You have taught me the difference between rape and making love when I didn't think anyone would ever want me. After I opened up to you that day in your car, I thought for sure I'd never see you again. You've surprised me at every turn.

You've opened up my eyes and changed my outlook on cops, sex, relationships, men and even tattoos...the list is endless. Your patience changed me. I am a better person because of you. I am attached. I feel like I belong and I understand my self-worth.

I've never wanted to see the world more than I do now, but I must leave you, the man who makes me feel alive, at the same time he takes my breath away. I love you so much and I'm terrified I'll never feel this way again. Should I have stayed? Should I have begged you to come with me? Will my mere existence consist of shattered pieces without you in it? I don't know.

I pray someday our paths cross again when the timing is right. If not, then you will always be the best thing I let get away. Thank you for the greatest summer I have ever had. I will cherish everything we've shared for as long as I live.

Until we meet again,

Clara Kate

I stared at the damp dots on the piece of paper from crying. They were sad tears mixed with happy ones. I am so much stronger now. I have come a long way in such a short period of time.

"Hey, babe," Jack said, startling me. I folded the piece of paper in half so Jack couldn't see how much I had written. "What are you doing?"

"Writing. Are you ready?"

"As I'll ever be."

"How many houses are we going to go see?"

"She's got six lined up today around town."

"Wow. Are you excited?"

"Oh yeah!"

We met Jezebel's sister right down the street at house number one. Her name was Rose and she was just as beautiful as Jezebel, a younger version. She had a different look to her as well...I think because her hair was much shorter, but you could tell she put a lot of time into looking good. I wondered what Jack thought about her.

She smiled brightly at Jack when she saw him, leaning in and kissing his cheek while they exchanged a hug. I didn't like her touching my man at all.

"This is my girlfriend, Clara Kate. Clara Kate, this is Jezebel's little sister, Rose."

Am I crazy or did Rose just frown at Jack's use of the term girlfriend? Hmmm...

I tried to ignore Rose's googly eyes for Jack as the day went on. *Why was I so jealous?* Because I was leaving soon and couldn't stop Rose from weaseling her way into Jack's heart if she tried. I've heard this story before, girl dumps guy so guy goes for girl's younger sister. *Ugh*! I could see it happening clear as day.

"So, I hear you're leaving," Rose said, while Jack walked the perimeter of house number four.

"Just a house sitting job and then I'll be back."

"Oh, Jack didn't mention you were returning. He made it sound like a permanent thing. Are you moving in with him when you return?"

"Definitely," I lied. "That's why he asked me to come along today. He wants to make sure I love the house as much as he does."

"That's great. How long have you guys been together?"

Umm...a few weeks?

"Three or four months."

"Wow. He didn't even mention he had a girlfriend until the other day and we talk all the time."

Really? About what?

"Probably doesn't want it to get back to Jezebel." I watched Rose nod her head.

"What do you think about this one?" Jack asked. I didn't know who he directed the question to, so I stuttered to answer.

"I...I love it!"

"You do? Me too! It's my favorite so far today."

"Shall we continue to the next two houses?" Rose asked.

"Sure," Jack replied.

We followed Rose as we drove to house number five.

"Jack, Rose just told me you two talk all the time. How come?"

"She just checks in on me to make sure I'm okay. It was nice at first, but now it's kind of annoying."

Phew!

"Just tell her to scram."

Jack chuckled.

"She was a good shoulder to lean on when Jezebel left me. I might need her again when you leave me too."

No!

I sat there pouting, but Jack never noticed. He trailed Rose down a long dirt driveway that lead to a smaller house. You couldn't see the house from the road because it was surrounded by tall trees.

"Now this is beautiful!"

"I don't know," I said. "I might like this one the best."

"Well come on, let's see inside first."

I watched Rose hit the digits on the lock box to get the key that would let us in. I walked around the farmers porch while I waited.

"Are you coming?" Jack asked, peering around the corner of the house.

The house was gorgeous, recently remodeled. The more I walked around, the more I fell in love. The icing on the cake was the enclosed inground pool in the backyard.

"You could swim all year round!" I exclaimed.

"This house is amazing. I can't believe it's within my budget."

"Well, the owners have located their next dream house and are more than eager to sell," Rose said.

"What do you think?" Jack asked, looking at me.

"I think I wouldn't even go see the next house because this is definitely it! I mean, the yard is smaller than what you wanted, but you are never home to maintain a yard so that might work in your favor."

"I think this one is it, Rose. I'm getting a good feeling about it," he told her.

"Shall I draw up an offer?" Jack looked at me, but I had nothing to say to him. I didn't have the answer. This was such an exciting time in Jack's life and the realization that I wasn't going to be a part of it was painful. The fact that I could have all of this and am choosing not to hurt even more.

"Let's go back to my office and talk numbers. We'll draw up a contract if everything looks good."

"Sounds great."

"Are you okay?" Jack asked as we drove to Rose's office.

"Yeah."

"You're awfully quiet."

"It's just weird helping you plan a life without me in it," I said quietly while looking out the window. "Not to mention Rose undressing you with her eyes every time she looks at you."

"Oh please. Rose is like a little sister to me."

"All you talked about is how Jezebel's beauty caught your eye. Rose looks just like her, Jack."

"I can't believe you are saying all of this. Don't you want me to move on? I mean, you're going to do the same."

"Yes. I just didn't think it would hurt this bad," I confessed, regretting the single tear I just let fall. *I was going to be broken without Jack, wasn't I? Shattered with scattered pieces...*

"I don't understand what more I could give you. I'll give you whatever you want, Clara Kate. Please."

I let the tears fall, quickly wiping them. I didn't want Rose to know I was crying.

"I have never even looked at another woman the way I look at you."

"Then why can't you just come with me?" I begged.

"You and I are in this little bubble and I love that bubble, but I have an entirely different world outside of you...of us. My son is buried here. I visit his grave every birthday, every Father's Day and the day he died. I love my job. I have the best co-workers and the greatest friends. My family is here. I can't leave that...I won't do it."

"Okay," I said, hoping he would stop talking.

"Okay, you're upset with me or okay you understand what I am saying?"

"I'm sorry I even asked you. It was selfish of me."

"I'm telling you that love is the most beautiful emotion you will ever feel. It transforms people...it changes them. Feeling loved can be the only thing that helps someone move from where they are to where they want to be. You don't just walk away from that!"

"I know," I said, thinking back to the words I wrote in my letter to Jack.

"I don't think you do," he said, taking the knife in my heart and twisting it.

When we got to Rose's office, I debated on whether or not to tell Jack I was just going to sit and wait in the car. *Grow up! Wipe your eyes and go support the man whose supported you!* I climbed out of the car, hoping Rose wouldn't notice my blotchy red eyes.

Rose looked at us and smiled as she welcomed us into her office, doing a double take. *Oh yeah, she knows I've been crying.*

"If you both could follow me this way," Rose said, leading us down the hall and into a room. "Have a seat right there and we'll get started."

Jack took my chair out for me, sitting down after I did. I wondered why he didn't pull Rose's chair out for her. Maybe he was trying to show me that he cared about me more than her. I felt like an immature teenager. *Oh wait, I was. Jack deserves better...*

"So I'll run through the contract with you. The house is listed for two-hundred and eighty-seven thousand. I don't think we should offer too much under this. I did a comp on the house and the listing price is reasonable. Also, it's a competitive market and it's only been on the market for a few days. How about we offer two eighty-two?"

"Two sixty-two."

"That's over twenty thousand less, Jack. You might insult them."

"I'll type up a letter telling them how much I loved their house. Besides, if they are eager to sell like you said, then they may take the bait."

"Okay..." she said, tilting her head like she didn't agree. This was all way over my head and a little bit overwhelming.

"We'll offer two sixty-two," she continued. "You have thirty-five thousand from the sale of your old home and twenty-five thousand in cash, correct?"

"I don't mind putting the thirty-five down on this next house, but let's do fifteen cash."

Holy shit! Thirty-five, plus twenty-five is sixty thousand dollars! Jack was rich!

"Out of that fifteen, I'll need a thousand now for a deposit and the listing realtor requires four, but that will be later on down the line if they accept your offer."

"Okay, great!"

"Awesome. Let me write this up and I'll be back in just a minute."

I sat at the table looking at Jack who was staring right back at me.

"This is all gibberish to me," I said. "But you on the other hand..."

"Well, this will be my second time. The first time I had no clue what was going on. I just signed on the dotted line."

"So how did you get all that money?"

"Well, the thirty-five is from my half of my first house and the twenty-five I saved all on my own."

"Wow, that's amazing!"

"Yeah, I want to pay this house off and retire early."

"Why?"

"I want to travel."

"The United States in an RV or something?"

"Sure, but I want to travel much more than that...like to London and Paris."

"Very funny. You're just saying that."

"I am not. Obviously I wanted to see the world at your age, but I had Jamison, so I had to start working right away to support him."

"As a police officer?"

"I was a dispatcher for a long time. That's what got me into wanting to be an officer. I was working the day my mother's call came in that Jamison was unresponsive. I just didn't personally get the call."

"That's crazy. I can't imagine receiving that phone call."

"Yeah. My good friend took it, he turned around in his chair and told me to go home...that he was dispatching first responders to my address."

I grabbed Jack's hand and kissed it. Rose entered the room and I suddenly felt awkward displaying my affection for Jack in front of her. I let go of Jack's hand, straightening up in my chair and scooting in closer to the table.

"So if all this looks okay, I just need you to sign and date the bottom. I typed up a letter for you. I hope you don't mind," she said, sliding the paperwork over to Jack. He took a moment to scan them over.

"Perfect," he said, smiling at her.

"Great. I will get this over to their listing agent right away and I'll let you know when I hear anything."

"You're the best, Rose," he said, standing up and grabbing my hand abruptly. I stood up and we walked through the door as Jack waved goodbye. When we got to Jack's car, I asked him what the heck that was all about.

"She was going to hug and kiss me again. I didn't want to upset you."

"I may be a little jealous, but I'm not crazy. Of course girls are going to be attracted to you, look at you!"

Jack chuckled.

"All I could think about while you two babbled was undressing you and riding you all night," I said. Jack stopped abruptly and turned towards me with his hand on his door handle.

"Clara Kate! You can't say stuff like that. At least wait until we get into the car," he said, glancing down at the bulge in his pants.

"What? Let's just do it right here like before." He shook his head. "Okay, fine...we can have sex inside your car. Is that better?"

"And give Rose a show when she comes out any minute now? Absolutely not!" he said, opening his door and climbing inside. I climbed inside next to him, deliberately running my tongue along my bottom lip to tease him.

"Fuck," he hissed, unzipping his pants before leaving the parking lot. I unbuckled my seatbelt, bending down and taking him into my mouth. "Seat belt stays on, Clara Kate. Do you know..."

I put my left hand over Jack's mouth to silence him while I used my right to buckle myself back up. Then I continued on my journey of giving road head for the first time. This was another story Jesse told me all about. Now I could actually understand what she was saying, about not understanding how a guy could drive and receive a blow job at the same time. I would surely crash when it came time to orgasm.

"Wow, that took a while," I said, after swallowing. My neck hurt like hell.

"Well I was trying to concentrate on driving, which wasn't easy," he said, as if I forced him into it.

"Oh please, you had your pants unzipped. Hmmm...I wonder what you wanted."

"I was just letting him breathe," he said, referring to his penis.

"Oh shut up. You loved it!"

"I did. I love you. You have such a hold over me."

"What do you mean?"

"Road head isn't legal. I heard about this guy a few years ago that got into a car accident. When first responders arrived, there was this woman pinned under the dash and the driver had his pants pulled down. Everyone knew what they were doing..."

"Did they both survive?"

"She did, but he didn't. He was probably orgasming, which is why he crashed."

"Wow."

"Now you see why you have a hold over me? I know it's wrong, but you make it feel so right."

"No. I'm saying wow because that's probably the best way to die. Death by orgasm."

Jack rolled his eyes at me.

"You love me!" I said, leaning over and kissing him on the cheek.

"I do...way too much."

We were quiet the rest of the ride home, both deep in thought. I wish I had this crystal ball that would show me my future. I knew this was going to go one of two ways. I leave and return or I leave forever. I wanted to leave forever, but part of me knew there was this chance I would return.

CHAPTER TWELVE

"Clara Kate," Jack said, standing in the doorway. He was brushing his teeth.

"What?" He had a very concerned look on his face. I stood up and walked to the bathroom, watching him spit into the sink and rinse off his toothbrush.

"What is it, Jack?"

"I just got a text from my friend. Michael committed suicide in his jail cell."

"When? How?"

"I don't know. I haven't asked."

"Give me your phone," I demanded, wanting to know answers.

"I'll call him," he suggested. I watched him on his phone.

"How'd he do it? Okay...do you know when? All right, that's all. Thanks man," he said, hanging up.

Jack let out a loud sigh and shook his head.

"It's gruesome."

I started to cry. I hated gruesome. All my life I hated Halloween and scary movies. I'd probably be having nightmares for weeks.

"I want to know."

"I don't want to tell you."

Jack brushed by me and climbed into bed. I followed him.

"I want to know, Jack," I pleaded, my eyes meeting his as we laid our heads down on our pillows simultaneously.

"I think it's time you stop digging and start protecting what's in here," he said, resting his hand on my head. I was already well aware I was never going to be able to erase any of this from my brain.

"Please," I urged.

I knew he was playing tug a war with his emotions right now and I loved him even more for wanting to protect me.

"He bashed his head against a concrete wall repeatedly."

I closed my eyes, picturing him. OH MY GOSH...what a horrible and painful way to die. I began to cry.

"When?"

"The minute he was placed back in his jail cell."

"The day I saw him?"

"Yes."

I curled up into a ball next to Jack and let go of every tear I held inside. The more I dug, the messier this was getting. There wasn't a shred of doubt in my mind that Mike would still be alive if I had never gone to see him. It didn't matter that this man was ill and filled with wicked. I could feel his blood on my hands now.

****

Jack tried to lift my spirits by deciding we should do something fun together every day until I left. He chose first and took me on a hot air balloon ride, which I absolutely loved. It made me realize that Jack was right. It was time I start safeguarding the thoughts in my head. Like everyone else, I only have this one life. I've heard countless times that life is incredibly short. I needed to take this time and try my hardest to make every moment treasurable. This was something I was going to have to work at. My mind was filled with notions I couldn't just turn off.

Throughout the week we had gone to a movie, then back to the sports complex we had gone to on our first date. Today was my day to choose and it was a no brainer. I wanted to go for a run with Jack.

Throughout our entire relationship he would never come for a quick run with me. I even gave up my daily jog on his days off.

"Run with me."

"You're kidding. I thought you would come up with something like a picnic or boat ride. This is supposed to be fun! Running? You want to get all sweaty together in the hot Missouri sun?"

"I've suggested going out to eat, but you said you enjoy cooking for me. You never come running with me."

"It's just not my thing."

"I get lonely. Besides, isn't that a requirement as a police officer to stay in shape?"

"Not with all the donuts we're supposed to eat."

"Very funny. I'm serious, I want to go for a run with you...it doesn't have to be long. A few miles?"

"Absolutely not. If you need exercise, we can take this running idea to the bedroom."

"Fine. One mile? I thought today was supposed to be my day to choose."

"Okay, Clara Kate. Let me go get my basketball shorts on and sweat my ass off after I just showered," he said, shaking his head and smirking.

I watched him walk down the hall to the bedroom. *What a big baby!* I finished lacing my sneakers and left without him.

Like the brat that I am, I headed right for Jack and Jezebel's street. We avoided his house like the plague when we walked Rocky, so surely he would never think to head in this direction. When I got to the end of the road, I hooked a right and headed down the street smirking to myself.

Suddenly I heard a car approaching and before I could turn around to see it, I felt a sharp pain in my elbow. I was thrown to the ground and rolled through the leaves down the embankment. I didn't have any time to think. When my body finally came to a stop, I laid there staring up at the sky. *What the hell just happened?*

My entire body ached, but most of the pain still resided in my elbow and now my knee. I didn't even want to look at the damage. I sat up and looked around. It was beautiful down here, untouched land for miles and miles. *Ugh, my knee. It's not bad...a bit bloody. I must've hit a stick on the way down.*

I stood up, unable to put a lot of pressure on my leg and limped up the hill on all fours. I unzipped the pocket on my shorts to get my phone and called Jack.

"Where the heck are you? This isn't funny anymore, Clara Kate."

I know...jokes on me.

"Can you come pick me up? I banged a right after I ran down your road."

"Are you okay? What's wrong?"

"I got hit by a car, but I'm okay."

"Jesus Christ! I'll be right there..." he said and hung up.

Oh no. I'm in trouble now.

"What happened? Where's the car?" he asked before I could even get into the passenger seat.

"I never saw it, but I think the vehicle was white. The driver just nudged my elbow."

"The car drove up onto the sidewalk?"

"No...I wasn't on the sidewalk. I just enjoy running along the woods better."

"That's exactly why there are sidewalks...so shit like this doesn't happen!"

Yeah...I know!

"Why are you so filthy?"

"There's an embankment."

"The car hit you so hard you flew down an embankment, but you're okay. Right...?" he grumbled as he drove on. "Why do you always do this? You just talk it down and talk it down. Being hit by a car is a big fucking deal. You could've been killed! You don't even have the courtesy to wait for me, so now you're out running alone not on a sidewalk when there's one five fucking feet away..."

"Enough!"

"I really don't understand how you think you're going to make it in some foreign country all by yourself..." he went on. I understood not running on the sidewalk was pretty careless of me, but I didn't need some father daughter speech right now. I was shaking with adrenaline. My nerves were shot and all I really wanted to do was to be coddled. Maybe I was just an adult child who was never going to make it on her own. I was going to prove Jack wrong.

When we parked in the driveway, I turned to face him.

"I don't want to do this with you anymore."

"This meaning us?" he asked.

"Yeah. I think it's best if you..."

"You're leaving in just a few days. Why can't we end things on a good note?"

"We can. I just think the pressure of knowing the inevitable is nearing is literally tearing us apart. I mean, I just got hit by a car and I realize it could've been a lot worse, but I'm still scared and the last thing I need is you lecturing me. I know you're mad at me...I get it, but that doesn't allow you to spend our last days together being angry. I need you to pack your things and leave."

Jack got out of the car without a word. I made sure I was one step ahead of him so I could unlock the door. I bowed my head and closed my eyes. "Please Jack...don't do that thing where you leave and come right back. I loved that then, but I just can't do it again." I opened the door and Jack brushed past me towards the hallway. I watched him pack his duffle bag as I stood in the doorway to the bedroom.

Stay strong. Stay strong!

I backed up into the hall as he brought his bag out and dropped it by the door. Then I watched him walk around the house gathering his various belongings. He reached up into the cabinet over the refrigerator and pulled out an envelope.

"My letter to you...if you still want it."

"Thank you," I said, taking it.

"I guess this is our goodbye," he said, standing by the door.

"Wait." I ran to the bedroom to retrieve my letter for Jack, hoping and praying he would read it when I was in London.

"Here...my letter to you."

"It's all a little pointless now...wouldn't you say? You're the one asking me to leave."

"Not at all. Please just take it and read it after I've left."

He opened up the front door. *No hug? Nothing?* I stood there completely shocked and then he turned back and looked at me.

"I wish I never met you," he said and closed the door.

Wow.

Jacks words hit me and they hit me hard. Through all the pain I have ever endured, I think those six words strung together hurt the most. Maybe because I didn't feel that way at all. Meeting Jack was the best thing that has ever happened to me and knowing we no longer shared this mutual feeling made my lungs feel airless.

"Hey girl!"

"Jesse!"

"What is it?"

"Something really bad just happened."

"What?"

"I just...I thought it would be better if Jack left. It's going to happen anyway so what does it matter?"

"Oh no..."

"I thought that it was going to be okay. Gosh I don't know what I was thinking now. I had to do it."

"So he's gone..."

"I told him to pack up his things and leave and he did."

"Did he even say anything?"

"Yes," I cried, not knowing if I could repeat his words.

"Oh, Clara Kate. I'll come home."

"You left?"

"Yesterday. I called you this past week, but it went to voicemail and you didn't call me back..."

Oh...right. Jack and I were...busy in bed so I sent your call to voicemail. I'm an awful friend...

"I wanted to see you before you left and I leave too."

"I'll come home this weekend. My last day of orientation is tomorrow and then by tomorrow night we will pig out on popcorn, ice cream and chick flicks. Okay?"

"Okay."

"If anyone knows how to heal from a nasty breakup it's totally me. You're in good hands," she laughed.

"Thanks Jesse."

"Don't mention it. See you tomorrow night."

****

"Wow! You look so...happy!" I gushed when I saw Jesse standing on the front step.

"I wish I could say the same for you."

"Yeah...sorry," I said. "I haven't showered today and well...I haven't even gotten out of my pajamas."

"That bad, huh?"

"Oh yeah," I said, sitting on the couch. Jesse followed and sat next to me.

"So, you want to tell me what happened?"

"If you promise not to blow any of what I tell you out of proportion."

"And I have done that..."

"I know. Never. Anyway, I was running yesterday and this car must not have seen me because it drove too close to me and clipped my elbow. It sent me into the woods and down into an embankment, BUT I'M OKAY..."

"He freaked out, didn't he?"

"Yes! He started playing dad with me which was so incredibly annoying."

"He cares about you! He's a police officer, Clara Kate. Keeping people safe is this guy's full-time job!"

"I know and I understand that, but he was so sweet when I met him and it was almost like the more my time here in Missouri was ending, the angrier he became. He went an entire week without talking to me. Then we'd be good for a couple days and then we'd argue again. I felt like I was on this emotional rollercoaster with him and honestly I didn't know how much more I could take."

"So you saw a way out and you took it?"

"Yeah...I guess."

"Well how do you feel?"

"Not good. I really thought I was going to be okay and then before he left, he said something to me."

"What did he say?"

I started crying.

"Sorry," I told her.

"Oh please. How many times have I come running to you? At least now it's nice we're on the same level here...I think."

"We are. We had sex."

"WHAT?" she shrieked.

"Yeah. The first time it didn't go very well, but he was gentle and patient. If I was broken, well, now I'm fixed."

I scooped my shirt up over my face and sobbed.

"Oh no," Jesse said, scooting closer and placing her arm around me. She began rubbing my back.

"He said he wished he never met me..."

"What? He said that?"

"It was the last thing he told me."

"No...he doesn't mean that. He's just angry."

"He meant it. I know he did," I cried on.

"But not in the way you're thinking. He truly loves you...nothing about your situation was easy. You two gave it your best shot and you rocked it with your first relationship. You've probably grown so much."

"I have..."

"Maybe you could just write him a letter to gain some closure. Having words left unsaid is never easy."

"I had a letter that I gave him before we broke up and he gave me one too. It was this cute idea we had."

"What does his say?"

"I'm going to wait until I'm in the air to read it. I'm afraid whatever he wrote will make me want to stay."

"Can I read it?"

I thought about her question for a moment. Surely it wouldn't do any harm to me now.

"Yeah, I guess. I just don't want to know anything it says just yet. Okay?"

"Okay."

I went and retrieved Jack's letter, dropping it in her lap. Then I sat there and watched her read it. It was one page, but the first page ran onto the back. I thought once or twice about trying to peek at the words, but my conscience knew better and so I looked away.

"Holy shit, girl!"

"What?"

"This guy...wow."

"What is it?"

"I'm just letting you know right now that this guy set you up for relationship failures."

"What? How?"

"Oh, you're never going to find someone to fill his shoes. They don't make 'em like this anymore. Well, maybe the men overseas are different."

"I don't think I want to find someone to fill his shoes. In fact, that'll be the last thing I even think about. Relationships are messy. There's too many emotions involved."

"Relationships are beautiful. Well, ones like these are," she said, holding up Jack's letter. "This stuff right here reminds me of my parents."

"What do you mean?"

"Well, I don't know how you two are together, but judging by this letter this is love...the truest kind. See, there's love and then there's true love. The regular generic love is a couple that says the 'I love you I love you, too' and then there's the true love when you walk by a table at a restaurant and this couple is sitting there. They're looking at each other smiling or maybe he's got his hand holding hers and you just feel it. There's no using words with the true love because his or her feelings are played out through physical assurance."

I sat there speechless.

"What?" Jesse smirked.

"Jesse, where did all of that just come from? You out of anyone I know has the worst taste in finding love!"

"Oh shut up!" she said, picking up a pillow and hitting me with it.

"Thanks for that," I laughed. "Maybe it knocked some sense into me."

"No...you have to go live out your dream. Don't think you're staying here just for your first love. Take this summer and learn from it. Grow! Go have fun in life."

"Maybe I should be saying these things to you..."

"Oh please, I'm in college now! I am going to have a blast this year."

"I'm going to miss you so much," I said, wrapping my arms around Jesse and squeezing as tight as I could. "I love you!" I kissed her on her cheek.

"Who are you and what have you done with my best friend?"

"Oh hush! I can love on my best friend before we part ways."

"We can FaceTime anytime you want," she said.

"You won't have time for me. Fraternities...keg stands...I know what you college kids do."

****

That weekend with Jesse was the best weekend I could ever remember having with her. We didn't do anything spectacular. We actually visited her grandmother in the nursing home, but I enjoyed every minute of it. When it was time for Jesse to go back to college, I cried.

"Are these tears for me, Clara Kate?" she asked, smiling.

"They sure are! I just couldn't ask for a better friend. You've stuck by my side through my dark, overweight phase and here you are with me through my first breakup."

"Can I ask you something?"

"Anything..."

"I've always wanted to know if you've ever found yourself suicidal. I never wanted to ask because I feared it would plant that thought inside your head."

"Well, I'm ashamed by the truth, but the answer is yes. Why do you ask?"

"My dad has this co-worker whose daughter just hung herself in their backyard. I guess she was sexually abused when she was eight and struggled coping with it."

"How old was she?"

"Fifteen."

"Wow."

"I know. It just got me thinking about you and everything you've been through. Sometimes I still worry about you...afraid that you'll go back. It was just really hard to watch," she said, tears forming in her eyes.

"Awww, are these tears for me, Jesse?" I asked, mirroring her own words to me.

"I just...I'm so thankful that if you ever felt suicidal you never actually followed through with it. What made you hold on?"

"You."

"Me?"

"Yes...you."

"What do you mean? How?"

"One time I was driving down the highway and I was thinking about going off the road and crashing my mom's car into a tree. You called and told me you had just won those concert tickets from the local radio station. Then remember that time you stopped by and found me in the shed?"

"Yeah. I was calling your name forever!"

"I was looking for rope to hang myself."

"WHAT?"

"That's not the only two times. It's like every time my mind started running with those dreadful ideas you were there to remind me to keep going." Jesse grabbed me and held on. I could feel her body trembling in my arms.

"Jesse...it's okay. I don't have those thoughts anymore. I promise!"

"It's just if you ever did that, I'd be heartbroken. You're my best friend. Oh God, thank you for never doing that to me."

"Thank you for always being there for me."

I watched Jesse drive away knowing I was going to miss her. If Jack and I had never broken up, I would've never spent this weekend reminding myself how special Jesse's friendship was to me. I think I had taken advantage of Jesse because at times I couldn't relate to her, but in the end that didn't really matter. What mattered was having someone you could call that would drop everything they're doing just to be with you.

I called my mother.

"Hello?"

"Hi, Mom. How are you?"

"Oh good. I've been so busy with work and helping your brother before he went back to college."

"You've got the house to yourself now!"

"Don't say that like it's a good thing. I miss my kids!"

I let out a small laugh.

"So are you still at the house with the chickens?"

"Yes! It was a great house. I'll definitely miss it."

"I hope you plan on seeing me before you go."

"Actually, I was going to ask if you could bring me to the airport in two days."

"Two days? Oh, honey...I have to work. Well what time were you thinking?"

"I'm taking the red eye to London, so not until nighttime."

"Okay. I can do that. Maybe I can take you to dinner before you go."

"I'd really like that."

My relationship with my mother became distant during my dark days in high school, so now I'll take advantage of bonding with the woman I once looked up to.

"I'll just come by when I get off. I'm going to go home and change first and then I'll pick you up. Okay? Let's say between five and six."

"All right, Mom. Thank you. I'll see you then."

"Okay. Goodbye, sweetie."

"'Bye."

****

I woke up with this feeling I got every time my time at a house was ending. It was this saying goodbye to the old and anticipating the new type of emotions. I was always excited for both. The ending was the most amount of work because I had to leave the house exactly the way I left it. Thankfully, I only had myself to pack up since Jack had already left.

What am I even saying? Thankful? No. Not at all. I'd be more thankful walking around the house picking up after him right now. I missed him. I wondered if he felt the same way. Did he close on his house? When would he be moving in there? *Oh no...don't do this. Don't start thinking about his life without you in it.*

I needed to see him one last time. I still had his police scanner, but I had every intention of taking it with me sort of as a souvenir...a well cherished keepsake. Maybe when I was able to part with it, it would mean I was finally over him.

I walked Rocky by his house the night before, but his car wasn't in the driveway. Today I'll walk Rocky in the mid-afternoon and hopefully catch Jack before he goes to work. I knew what time he usually left.

I leashed up Rocky and laced my feet. *Please be home. Please be home*. What does one say to somebody who tells them "I wish I never met you."

Oh, hey there...

No.

I just wanted to say goodbye.

No! We already did that.

Please come with me.

No, no, no...

And then I looked up and there was his car driving towards me. I stopped and pulled Rocky back. My eyes followed his vehicle the entire time and when he drove past me, he looked right into my eyes.

No!

He kept driving. *Please, please stop*! I wanted so badly to see brake lights, but I never did. I couldn't believe we were ending things like this. The first man I had ever said I love you to. The first man to tell me that HE loved me and now just like that he's gone.

I wanted to call him. I wanted to text him, but deep down I knew he had made his decision and now I must live with mine.

CHAPTER THIRTEEN

"I'm going to miss you, my baby girl," my mother said, sitting across from me at the dinner table. *This was weird*. This was really weird! I can't remember the last time my mother called me her baby girl.

As I sat there, I wanted so badly to ask her about my father. I wanted to tell her he was dead. Maybe she already knew. I wanted to tell her all about my visit with Uncle Mike and what she thought about him committing suicide within hours of seeing me. But I didn't know where that might lead us and tonight, I just wanted to have a good night with my mom.

The smile in her eyes for me was sincere and I enjoyed every minute of it.

"I'll miss you, too! I'll write to you. Maybe we can be pen pals!"

"I'd really like that. Call me anytime too."

"I know. It's just, with the time change and you always working, a pen pal relationship might work really nicely."

"I agree," she said.

"You haven't mentioned Jack at all," she said, on the ride to the airport.

"Things didn't end so well. I'll probably cry if we talk about it."

"I think he's really fond of you, sweetheart."

"I think you're right," I said, looking out the window. I wanted to remember everything about Missouri before I leave.

"Sometimes I wonder if I'll ever feel as loved by anyone else. He made me feel like I could conquer the world. Do you think love is something that is hard to find?"

"Hmmm...well, do you want me to be honest? I mean, I don't want to stop you from leaving tonight."

"Why? I mean, it was you who hated my idea the most."

"I was just upset. I mean, I understand I never asked which college you narrowed it down to and that was bad parenting on my part, but every time I did ask about anything to do with it you would get such an attitude with me."

"I know. I'm sorry, Mom. I just know inside my heart this is what is right for me at this point in my life."

"I understand that."

"I've done the whole school thing the last twelve years of my life and I hated it."

"Especially high school."

"And maybe someday I'll go to college, Mom. I'm not ruling it out entirely. Just right now I am."

"Okay. Now can I answer your question?"

"Yes."

"I think truthfully that you only find one true love."

"But how will I know if it was Jack?"

"Oh, honey. You'll know. I haven't met anyone that ever compared to your father. He was it for me."

"Really? You can honestly say that even after separating from him?"

"Yes. I really can. I loved him dearly."

"That's really sad, Mom."

"It depends on what way you look at it. He gave me some of the best years of my life and then he gave me three beautiful kids to top it off. Maybe I'll even be a grandmother again someday."

"How come you thought that what you had with Dad was truly love?"

"Well for starters, I was infatuated with him. We did everything together and enjoyed one another tremendously. It wasn't just all the happy moments though. Even our fights were passionate. He'd get so angry with me because he loved me so much. You can only pull all sorts of those emotions out of someone who truly loves you."

"I never thought of love in that sort of way. Wow..." I said, as we drove along. "I think this thing with Jack was love, the real kind, but I wasn't willing to risk being wrong. Do you think that makes me a selfish person?"

"No. Not at all. I think you made the right decision. If it's meant to be, it'll be."

"Thanks, Mom."

I hugged my mother goodbye and headed to check-in. I had an hour to kill before I boarded the plane. I took Jack's letter out and placed it on my lap. I looked down, staring at it and thinking about all my relationships. After everything that happened this summer, I was so happy to be leaving on a good note with both my mother and Jesse.

A single tear ran down my cheek as I thought again about my relationship with Jack. *This is it. No turning back. Well, I could turn back at the end of this contract in three months, but would Jack take me back with open arms?* He told me time and time again that I could go back to him no matter what. *No. He wouldn't take me back this time.*

I started feeling more and more nervous as I boarded the plane. I think I was more nervous about reading this damn letter than my actual flight. I waited until I was in the air to tear the letter open. Thanks to Jesse already reading it, I slid the piece of paper out...

Dear Clara Kate,

I have a story for you...

Once upon a time there was this guy named Jack. He was this all-star quarterback. All the girls loved him, including the hottest cheerleader on the squad. She was older than him, which made him want her even more. Jack thought he had the life until the day she

placed a positive pregnancy test in his hand. His heart was filled with anger and resentment.

The door closed on his first high school sweetheart and another one opened on the first day he held his newborn son. He gave him his very own name, Jamison Ray McDonald. It was love at first sight and from that day on, Jamison became Jack's motivation. Jack finished high school, got a full-time job right after graduation and worked his butt off to become a police officer. Some days he wanted to give up, but the sweet voice of Jamison, "I love you, Daddy," was all it took to keep him going.

They say when one door closes another will open. Sadly, Jamison's door closed on June 9th, 2017, Jack's mother's birthday. That day is no longer one that is worth celebrating in the McDonald family. It's a day of agony and heartbreak.

Jack's door opened again within the first year to a beautiful young woman named Jezebel. Jack had never seen anyone quite like her. She was...exotic. Jezebel had just finished paying for her coffee and when she turned to see Jack standing there in line in his uniform, she told the cashier she would pay for his too. They got to talking and Jack thought early on she was the one.

Jack always went for a woman of beauty, but he never took the time to find out what was inside their heart. When Jezebel walked away after three years of commitment and a ten-thousand-dollar diamond ring, Jack swore he would never be lured by looks again.

Fourteen days later, still nursing a broken heart, Jack came face to face with a young woman by the name of Clara Kate. Right away there was something that caught his eye. She possessed this certain kind of beauty Jack had never known. She wasn't wearing a touch of makeup; her hair was a mess and yet she was breathtaking, but she held this unexplained fear in her eyes. Jack could feel it too.

Jack had only ever been lured by the ladies, but not by Clara Kate. From that day forward, she became an impulse in his heart. He had to see her. He needed to be with her. In her own refined way,

Clara Kate was delicate and Jack realized early on that she was clueless on how exquisite she truly was.

Clara Kate began to change and Jack started realizing he was changing too. She became confident, fearless and downright extraordinary. Jack knew the last time he had felt this way about anyone was the first day he held his baby boy.

I must end this story here because this story has no ending. See, you can never rewrite the beginning, but you can always start now and make a brand new ending. There's a door for Jack and Clara Kate. She can open it or she can close it. You write this story's ending for me...

Jack

Wow! The voice inside my head was speechless. I grabbed a tissue from my purse, wiping my eyes and read the letter again. *Holy shit*! Jack was a writer...a good one. Jack and Clara Kate were captivating. I was reading a story about myself that I didn't want to end.

It felt strange learning something new about Jack, someone I felt closest to. Jamison was his name. I wonder if he changed it to Jack after his son passed, not wanting to feel the pain in his heart every time he heard his own name.

I scanned the letter again, picking out the words he used to describe me: delicate and exquisite. I scanned some more finding confident, fearless and extraordinary. I was most definitely delicate when we met, but Jack made me into all of those wonderful words he wrote. There was no replacing him.

I looked to the front of the plane and I knew just what I wanted to do if I could do it. I'd tell the captain to turn this plane around.

CHAPTER FOURTEEN

When the plane finally landed, I was exhausted. I didn't even know what time it was. I immediately got out of my seat to retrieve my luggage from the overhead cab, noticing everyone was watching me as they remained seated. I sat back down, realizing the front of the plane was exiting first.

Right.

"First time flying," I explained to the man next to me. He just smiled without a word.

I exited the plane, wanting to scoot by everyone in front of me. *Why were they going so slow? Why am I in such a rush?* There was nowhere I had to be. I was just so excited and scared all at the same time, but a good scared. I was ready to see an entirely different world!

I followed everyone to the luggage claim. I stood there and waited impatiently. After what felt like forever, I saw my giant pink suitcase making its way along the belt. I knew how heavy it was and I started feeling nervous I wasn't going to grab it in time or I would go to pick it up and struggle like a defenseless kitten. *All right, you got this Clara Kate, here it comes*. Just as I went to grab the handle, somebody swooped in and grabbed my bag. Ready to demand my luggage back, I turned to see Jack. I let out a shriek, barely able to catch my breath and began crying, knowing Jack had been on the same plane as I was this entire time.

"What are you doing?" I asked, my voice shaking.

"I couldn't do it."

"Do what?"

"Let our story end."

I looked around, quickly realizing all eyes were on us.

"What about your job?"

"I took an extended leave of absence."

"Nooo," I said, my voice filled with worry. I know how much Jack loves his job.

"Your family. What about them?"

"My parents gave me their blessing, Clara Kate. My mother practically pushed me out the door and told me to follow my heart."

"You love being a police officer, though. Not to mention your visits to Jamison's grave? I-I-I can't let you give all that up for me, even if only for the time being."

"You're not hearing me, though," he said, grabbing my two hands and pulling me closer. "It's you that I can't give up. Sure, the details aren't quite figured out yet and maybe I'm being selfish just leaving so suddenly, but I do know that the thought of living life without you in it, well, I just can't. Maybe we'll go back home in a couple of months, after your house sitting job. Or we'll stay for a while longer and make a decision after that..."

I opened my mouth to speak and closed it again. The truth was, Jack didn't need to explain these almighty emotions because I felt them too.

"There's nothing you can say right now that's going to get me on a plane back home," he said, grabbing my face and holding it between his two warm hands. "You pulled these feelings out of me, feelings that should've died with my last relationship. You inspired this unconditional love I thought I'd only ever have for Jamison."

His eyes looked teary now, the way they always had when he spoke about his beloved son.

"I have the best job in the world and the most loving family," Jack leaned in closer to me, lowering his voice to a whisper. "I have enough savings to carry me through this leave of absence, but what does any of it really mean if I don't have my Clara Kate?"

THE END

ABOUT THE AUTHOR

Born on October 1, 1987, in Boston, Massachusetts, I grew up in Plymouth where I was encouraged to write in my very first diary given to me by my mother at age nine. It was then I found my love for writing. I still reside on the east coast with my husband, five children and several farm animals. When I'm not typing away on my keyboard, you can find me in the kitchen cooking up something delicious! I also love crafting, gardening, reading, spending time with my family, venturing outdoors and camping.

I love to hear from readers via comments or emails. I answer personally at this e-mail address:

indiegirld.duquette@gmail.com

You can also add me on Facebook, @AuthorD.Duquette

Made in the USA
Columbia, SC
05 August 2022